FOOL'S CHALLENGE

"You have a hearing problem, mister?" Packard rasped. "I said find your horse and ride."

Munson's expression turned malevolent. "Why do I have to leave town when I killed this guy in a fair fight?"

Rubbed raw by the greenhorn's arrogance, the lawman snapped, "Because there's enough trouble and bloodshed in this town without itchy-fingered gunslingers hanging around. Now vamoose."

Sneering, Munson crowed, "So you know I'm a gunfighter, eh? Heard my name?"

"Nope. You just have that look about you. I've seen your kind a thousand times. Most of you don't last past three shoot-outs."

"I'm not like the rest of them fools," Munson declared. "Matter of fact, I'm more a match for the famous sheriff of Esmerelda County." Holstering his gun, he ordered, "Go for your gun, Packard."

The Badge Series
Ask your bookseller for the books you have missed

THE BADGE: BOOK 22

★

GUN TRAP

★

Bill Reno

 Created by the producers of
The Holts: An American Dynasty,
Stagecoach, and **White Indian.**

Book Creations Inc., Canaan, NY • *Lyle Kenyon Engel, Founder*

BANTAM BOOKS
NEW YORK • TORONTO • LONDON • SYDNEY • AUCKLAND

GUN TRAP

A Bantam Domain Book / published by arrangement with
Book Creations, Inc.

Bantam edition / April 1991

Produced by Book Creations, Inc.
Lyle Kenyon Engel, Founder

DOMAIN and the portrayal of a boxed "d" are trademarks of
Bantam Books, a division of Bantam Doubleday Dell Publishing
Group, Inc.

ISBN 0-553-28912-8

Published simultaneously in the United States and Canada

Bantam Books are published by Bantam Books, a division of Bantam
Doubleday Dell Publishing Group, Inc. Its trademark, consisting of
the words "Bantam Books" and the portrayal of a rooster, is
Registered in U.S. Patent and Trademark Office and in other
countries. Marca Registrada. Bantam Books, 666 Fifth Avenue,
New York, New York 10103.

PRINTED IN THE UNITED STATES OF AMERICA

OPM   0 9 8 7 6 5 4 3 2 1

GUN TRAP

★ BADGE ★

After gold was discovered in 1849, the dream of finding a fortune lured adventurers westward. Many techniques for obtaining gold were employed, from panning in streams to burrowing out honeycombed tunnels supported by timbers. One method used a cradle, which filtered out stones, allowing sand and gold to pass onto a canvas apron. As the sand washed down the apron, some gold adhered to it, and the rest was caught by slats of wood. The device was set on rockers and operated by a team, with one man rocking the cradle while others dug.

❖ BADGE 22: GUN TRAP ❖

Chapter One

A brisk wind was carried with the spring dawn down off the mountains that surrounded Aurora, Nevada. It whistled through the town and rushed into the inch-wide space between the window and sill of Sheriff Jess Packard's room at the Sierra Hotel, disturbing the curtains and awakening the sleeping lawman.

Running his fingers through his dark brown curly hair, Packard squinted at the window, then doubled the pillow under his head and cupped his hands behind his neck, interlacing his fingers. The cool air that toyed with the curtains was invigorating, although the sheriff was reluctant to leave the warmth of his bed.

Finally, knowing the desk clerk would arrive soon with hot water, Packard rose from the bed and slipped into his pants. Yawning and stretching, he padded to the window, parted the dancing curtains, looked down on Pine Street, Aurora's main thoroughfare, and surveyed his town.

Hearing hoofbeats and the rattle of a vehicle, he looked in the direction of the sound, and when the vehicle came into view, Packard saw it was the hearse. The undertaker was on his way to Boot Hill to bury three men. Two were drifters who had shot and killed each other the night before in one of the saloons; the third was a greenhorn gunslinger who had made the

1

same fatal mistake as many men had before him: He thought he could outdraw the seasoned Packard.

A light rap at the door pulled the tall, muscular man away from the window. Hurrying across the room, he called, "Willie?"

"Yep, it's me, Sheriff," came the muffled reply.

Packard opened the door and greeted Willie Bender. The clerk carried a small pail of steaming water to the washstand that already held a pitcher of cool water and a basin. His morning chore then completed, Bender left.

Stepping to the table, the lawman eyed his reflection and rubbed the day-old stubble on his angular face. He appraised his thick hair and trim mustache, deciding he did not need to see the barber as yet.

His gaze strayed from the mirror to the calendar that hung on the adjoining wall. Bold letters at the top announced the year was 1864, while slightly smaller letters indicated that the month was May. Putting a finger on Wednesday the eleventh, Packard looked at the small square on the bottom denoting June. Sunday, June 26, was circled. He smiled, saying audibly, "Just forty-six more days, Monica, darling. Forty-six days and you'll be Mrs. Jess Packard."

The handsome, thirty-one-year-old Packard had been sheriff of Esmeralda County, Nevada, since November 1860, the same year the tough mining town was founded. When an abundance of gold and silver was discovered, the county boomed fast. Like powerful magnets, the mines that dotted the landscape and the wealth they had produced drew claim jumpers, outlaws, gamblers, brawlers, and gunfighters. Along with them came trouble . . . and plenty of it. Aurora's responsible citizens had felt the need for a tough-handed sheriff.

When still only in his late twenties, Jess Packard had already cut his lawman's notch as town marshal of

Wichita, Kansas. Known to be as tough as old harness leather and faster than lightning with the Colt .45 on his hip, he was known in Nevada before he arrived, and when it was time for Esmeralda County to hire a sheriff, he was made an exceedingly attractive offer. It was an added incentive for him that his younger brother Alex lived in Aurora.

The tall, rugged lawman lathered his face, stropped his straight-edge razor a few licks, and began to shave. His thoughts strayed to the greenhorn he had been forced to kill the night before and then to all the deaths he had witnessed in Aurora during the past four years. He could not even recall how many men had been murdered in cold blood during that time, let alone those who had been killed in gunfights and brawls.

Washing the soap off his face, Packard put on a clean shirt and picked up the sheriff's badge from the dresser top and pinned it on. He then removed his gunbelt from the bedpost and strapped it around his slender waist, once again stepping to the window as he tied the holster down, his dark brown eyes assessing the town. He could hardly remember a day when there had not been bloodshed of some kind, and he wondered what violence the new day would bring.

Nestled among several mountains at an elevation of 7,500 feet, Aurora was only five miles from the California border and so close to the towering Sierra Nevadas that the majestic snow-covered spires of that range were in plain view. Now the county seat, Aurora had a population of well over five thousand, predominantly men. Including the "soiled doves" who had moved into the south end, only about three hundred women graced the town, and there were fewer than a hundred children.

The town boasted two daily newspapers, the *Esmeralda Union* and the *Aurora Times*, two stagecoach lines, eight hundred houses or cabins, and some three hundred commercial buildings—including twenty-five saloons and gambling houses. The rugged terrain around Aurora was dotted with miners' shacks and mills, and the streets were crowded daily with wagons carrying freight over the Sierra Nevadas from California on the Sonora Pass trail. Small numbers of Monache, Paiute, and Mojave Indians were visible, since a truce had been called between whites and Indians a year before—a truce that Packard had labored hard to bring about.

The lawman turned from the window, and after checking the loads in his revolver and holstering it, he donned his hat and stepped into the hallway. Locking the door, he descended the stairs and strode across the lobby out to the street, where his deputies—Neil Thurston, Al Cunningham, Lee Austin, and Ed Murdock—were waiting for him.

Lee Austin, the youngest of the four, flashed his winning smile and asked, "Sleep well, Sheriff?"

"Well enough," Packard replied. "Let's eat."

Walking a half block to the Sagebrush Café, the lawmen entered and occupied its largest table. While eating breakfast, Packard ran his gaze over the stalwart young faces of his men and stated, "Today we'll rotate sections. Specifically, Ed, you'll work the east side of town; Lee, you're on the north; Al, that puts you on the west; and Neil, if you're awake this morning, you can figure out where that puts you."

Thurston grinned and replied, "Uh-huh. The toughest part of town."

Laughing, Packard responded, "Yeah. And do the rest of us a favor and try to keep it as peaceful as—"

"Sheriff! Sheriff!" bellowed a middle-aged man as he barged through the door. "We got trouble out on the street!"

Muttering under his breath, Packard groused, "They

can't even let a man eat his breakfast." Sighing, he stood and asked, "What is it, Harvey?"

"One of them miners has got your future father-in-law down and is about to beat him up!"

The sheriff's chair fell over as he shoved it back and bolted for the door, with the deputies and Harvey following. Rushing outside, he found a small crowd collected around the two men who were in the middle of the street. Packard pushed his way past the onlookers to find Derek Wood, publisher of the *Aurora Times,* flat on his back with an enormous, burly miner astride him. Wood, in his early fifties and quite small, was covering his face with his arms as huge Dick Weaver roared, "I want your word on it right now, Wood, or I'm gonna pound you to a bloody pulp!"

Standing nearby, her face devoid of color, was Monica Wood, the publisher's blond, twenty-six-old daughter, who was Packard's fiancée. Beside her was Alex Packard, the lawman's younger brother, who worked for Wood.

Packard's face became as red as ox blood. Striding over to the miner, he ordered, "Get off him, Weaver!"

Weaver turned his own fury-reddened face on the sheriff and growled, "Not until he promises to print a retraction of that story about me in this morning's paper!"

"What story?"

"About me beatin' up that guy on Monday. You know, the one you chewed on me about 'cause he was littler than me."

"Well, you did beat him up!" Packard snapped with exasperation. "So Mr. Wood printed the truth in his paper."

"He didn't either!" bawled Weaver. "He wrote that I beat that guy up over a gamblin' debt. Now, that's a bald-faced lie! It was over a *woman.*"

Packard sighed again. He looked down at the publisher and asked, "Mr. Wood, where did you get your information about the fight being over a gambling debt?"

"From the man who was beaten up," came the reply.

"In all fairness, sir," said Packard, "you shouldn't have printed the story without hearing Weaver's side of it." Glaring again at the miner, he added coldly, "And you shouldn't have beaten that miner in the first place, him being only half your size."

"Yeah? Well, like I told you when you lit into me about it, he may not be very big, but he's got a big mouth."

"Well, it's over and done with now," Packard said. "Let Mr. Wood up"—his tone sharpened—"immediately."

Weaver set his jaw and stubbornly declared, "Not until he tells me he's gonna print a retraction."

"Look," retorted Packard, feeling his blood temperature rise, "it's over and done. The people who read the paper don't care what the fight was about. Now, let Mr. Wood up!"

Enraged, the big miner ignored the directive and smashed Wood's face, stunning him. Packard immediately snatched Weaver by the collar, yanking him off the publisher, and threw him on his back. Swearing profusely, Weaver scrambled to his feet and boomed, "Ain't no man gonna handle me like that! Not even a tin star!"

Pointing a stiff finger, Packard declared, "You'd better cool down quick, or you'll get yourself locked up!"

Like a maddened bull, the huge man went after the sheriff, fists balled, but the lawman easily ducked the punches, dug his heels in the dirt for leverage, and smashed the massive man on the jaw. The punch took Weaver by surprise, and his head whipped to one side as he reeled from its impact.

The crowd scrambled to the boardwalks while Alex

Packard—a smaller, sandy-haired version of his older brother—dragged the dazed publisher to safety.

Dick Weaver's back slammed against a wagon that was parked on the side of the street. He shook his head to clear his vision and vowed, "You're gonna get yourself whipped good for that, Sheriff!"

Bracing his feet, Packard rejoined heatedly, "Cool off and forget this whole thing, or you'll end up behind bars!"

The big man was deaf to Packard's warning, and he came at the sheriff with the obvious intent of destroying him. But Packard batted away both fists and planted a punch on Weaver's cheekbone. It was a glancing blow, however, and did not slow the giant down.

Suddenly a huge, meaty fist caught the sheriff solidly on the jaw, and he slammed against the ground. Lying on his back with the breath knocked out of him momentarily, he looked up to see the miner's huge form descending upon him like a giant carnivorous bird.

Packard rolled out of the way in the nick of time, and Weaver landed hard. As Weaver was getting up, Packard leapt to his feet and glanced at his deputies standing close by. They were clearly ready to jump in and help, but Packard shook his head. He would handle the monster all by himself.

The combatants closed in and traded blows. First one man seemed to be winning, but then the tide turned and the other appeared the victor for a while. Finally, the lawman landed solid blows to the miner's face, smashing his nose to a bloody pulp. But though Dick Weaver was battered and bleeding, his massiveness alone gave him formidable power, and he went after his smaller opponent with murder in his eyes.

The miner sent a hard blow to Packard's left ear, and the lawman backtracked, a roar setting up in his head. Laughing triumphantly, his adversary snarled and closed in for the kill. But Packard ducked the huge, deadly fist and drove a vicious punch to Weaver's jaw, momentarily slowing him, then quickly dug a fist into the big man's midsection, doubling him over. Slowly but steadily gaining the upper hand, Packard threw three more punches in rapid succession, striking Weaver's jaw and battered, tender nose.

Again Weaver rallied and countered with blows of his own, but the lawman came right back. The duration of the contest was taking its toll, however, and the two men gasped for air. Packard saw that the giant's stamina was waning, but his own would not last much longer against the man's sheer strength. He had to finish him quickly.

Avoiding two more potentially bone-crushing blows, the lithe sheriff peppered Weaver's mangled nose several more times with driving, savage blows. Jess Packard was like a woodsman, chopping at a giant tree, while Dick Weaver's strength was failing fast.

Finally Packard slugged Weaver three more times, stunning him, and the massive man's arms dropped to his sides. Planting his feet, the lawman drew back his right fist and put all of his weight into it, slamming it into his foe's jaw. The impact drove pain all the way from Packard's fist to his ankles, but it was the blow that finished the fight. The miner's knees buckled and gave way; then he fell to the street and lay there motionless, out cold.

The crowd erupted with a cheer for the sheriff. While Packard stood over his toppled opponent, sucking air into his lungs, his deputies gathered around him, praising his fighting ability. Monica left her father's side and dashed to Packard, gasping, "Oh, Jess! I was so afraid he was going to hurt you!"

Joining the couple, Alex smiled proudly and remarked,

"I told you Jess would handle him, Monica. I haven't seen the man yet that my brother can't whip!"

Packard bent over to pick up his fallen hat and, dusting it against his leg, said wryly, "Well, do me a favor and don't scour up any more like him for me to beat, Alex." Looking at his deputies, the lawman suggested, "You boys go back and finish your breakfast. I'll take Weaver to the jail and lock him up. He's going to spend a week as our guest for disobeying and striking an officer of the law."

Lee Austin spoke up. "I'll help you, Sheriff."

Packard nodded, then turned to Monica and asked, "Is your father okay?"

"He'll be fine, darling," she replied. "Thanks to you. That horrible man would have hurt him seriously if you hadn't come to the rescue."

"Just doing my job," Packard responded with a loving smile, giving Monica's shoulder an affectionate squeeze. He then signaled to his deputy, taking hold of the miner's wrists while Austin grabbed his ankles, and the two lawmen carted the unconscious Weaver down the street to the jail. Hauling the miner's bulk inside, they unceremoniously dumped him on the cot in the cell just as the man began stirring. The lawmen scurried out of the cell and locked it behind them, ignoring the curses issuing from Weaver's mouth.

"You can't leave me here!" Weaver howled.

"Oh, yes, I can," Packard rejoined. "For seven days, to be exact. That's your sentence for disobeying me and striking me."

"But I ain't seen no judge!"

Packard laughed. "You'd be in here a whole lot longer if I kept you locked up till he returned. He's not due back in Aurora for another three weeks."

While Weaver continued to shout choice epithets, the sheriff ushered his deputy out of the cell area, suggesting, "Let's go back and finish our breakfast, Lee."

A half hour later, Jess Packard appeared at the office of the *Aurora Times*. The bells on the door jangled when the lawman entered, and Alex Packard waved to his brother from across the room at the printing press. Derek Wood, who was at his desk, poring over a stack of mail, looked up and smiled weakly.

"How are you feeling, sir?" Packard asked as he reached the publisher's desk.

"I'll be all right, son," Wood replied. "I'm beholden to you for rescuing me from that monster—and I'll be plenty proud to have you as my son-in-law."

Monica came out of her private office just then and, hearing her father's words, laid a hand on her fiancé's arm. "I'll be even prouder to have you as my husband, darling," she cooed, then stood on her tiptoes and kissed him softly on the cheek.

Clearly embarrassed by the praise, Packard stated modestly, "Like I said before, I was just doing my job. After all, I'm supposed to protect people in this county from troublemakers."

"Nonetheless," Wood allowed, "I appreciate all you did. And incidentally, I *was* wrong to print the story without hearing Weaver's side. Should I print another article and say the fight was over a woman, not a gambling debt?"

"I think it would be best just to leave it alone, sir," Packard replied. "Besides, what difference does it make?"

"None, I guess. The only reason I printed the story at all was because I was needing some news yesterday."

Grinning, Packard remarked, "Well, if you need some news today, don't make it the most recent fight, okay? Word will spread all over the county fast enough as it is."

"Okay," Wood promised.

Kissing Monica on her forehead, Packard told her, "See you later."

Father and daughter watched the sheriff's retreating form. When he was gone, they smiled at each other, and Wood said, "Honey, you sure have chosen wisely. I'm pleased that you're marrying Jess. He'll bring a great deal of prestige to our family—and his esteem is well deserved."

The lovely blonde smiled and responded, "All my friends are green with envy, telling me what a good catch I've made." Giggling, she added, "And they're right." She hugged her father's shoulders and exclaimed, "Just think, in less than two months I'll be Mrs. Jess Packard, wife of the West's most famous lawman! It'll be a dream come true!"

It was just before noon when the Wells Fargo stage pulled up in front of Sheriff Jess Packard's office and stopped. Turning his attention from the paperwork on his desk to the open doorway, Packard could see that the six-up team was foamy and sweaty. Wondering why the stage had stopped in front of his office rather than proceeding down the street another block to the Fargo office, the lawman rose from his chair and started toward the doorway. When he got closer, he saw the body lying on top of the stage in the rack. Getting closer still, he saw that the dead man was Webster Kirgan, co-owner of the Young America mine just outside of Aurora.

The elderly driver, Cabel McKay, swung down hurriedly from his seat, while the young shotgunner, Robby Lyons, remained up in the box, his face pale. "Sheriff!" gasped McKay as he leapt across the boardwalk. "Web Kirgan is dead!"

"I can see that," Packard acknowledged as more people began gathering around the stage. Frowning, he asked, "How did it happen, Cabel?"

McKay's eyes were wild. Rubbing a nervous hand across his wrinkled, weathered face that had not been shaved in at least four days, he explained, "We were about six miles below Sonora Pass when three masked men bolted outta the timber. They forced me to stop the stage and made us throw our guns down, then ordered Mr. Kirgan to get out. They knew he was on the stage, that's for sure. Kirgan was pretty nervous about gettin' out, but he did what they told him. Then they killed Kirgan in cold blood . . . just cut him down without mercy and rode off."

Shaking his head in disgust, Packard stepped past the driver, nodded abruptly at the passengers who stared at him from inside the coach, and climbed up to the rack. After examining the body closely, he climbed down and remarked, "Looks like they put enough lead in him to kill a bull elephant. Tell me, was there anything familiar about the bandits?"

"Nope. Like I said, they was masked."

"I know that, but did you recognize clothing or horses?"

"Nope. Neither Robby nor me could pick out nothin' familiar at all. We talked about it right after they rode away." Gesturing at the stage, he added, "And the passengers are all strangers to these parts."

Rubbing his chin, the sheriff said, "Okay. Take Web to the funeral parlor, will you?"

"Yeah. I just thought I should let you know before we went any farther into town."

"I appreciate it, Cabel," Packard responded. "How soon are you supposed to pull out for another run?"

"Three days."

"Okay. I may need you and Robby to take a look at a few men today or tomorrow. You'll be at the hotel?"

"Yep. If me and Robby ain't there, we'll be at the Stockade Saloon, keepin' our whistles moist."

There was a low murmur among the crowd as the stage moved on down the street. They knew, as did Packard, that Webster Kirgan's killing might well spark more bloodshed. Recently there had been heated claims disputes between the two biggest local mines, the Young America and the Winnemucca, which were adjacent to each other. With the dispute getting hotter, Winnemucca owner Art Uzelac had hired six gunmen a few days ago as strong arms for his mine operation. Virgil Troop, the Young America's co-owner, was going to be more than red-hot over his partner's murder. Packard shuddered. *Real* trouble was brewing now.

Chapter Two

Stepping into the office, Deputy Sheriff Ed Murdock looked at the lawman behind the desk and asked, "You wanted to see me, boss?"

"Yeah," Jess Packard confirmed, nodding. "I sent for Al, too. As soon as he gets here, I'll explain the picture to both of you."

When Deputy Al Cunningham arrived, Packard informed them of Webster Kirgan's murder, relaying the details as stage driver Cabel McKay had given them. The deputies exchanged a glance, then Cunningham grumbled, "Looks like even more trouble's up ahead."

Murdock queried, "Do you think it was Uzelac's hired strong arms who killed Kirgan?"

"That's my first inclination," Packard answered. "Ed, you and I are going to the Winnemucca to talk to Art. I expect him to deny it, but I've got to give him the chance. If he does deny it, we'll have his new men parade themselves and their horses in front of McKay and Robby Lyons. If they recognize them, there'll be some arrests made immediately."

"Could get sticky," Murdock said levelly. "Maybe we ought to get Lee and Neil."

"No, I don't want to leave the town without protection," Packard replied. "The two of us will have to handle it ourselves." Rising and rounding the desk, Packard continued, "Al, while we're at the Winnemucca,

I want you to go to the Young America office and inform Virgil Troop that his partner's been murdered. He's going to be madder than a wet hen when he hears it, but don't let him do anything foolish. Tell him I've gone to talk to Art, and I'll come see him as soon as I'm finished."

Twenty minutes later, the three lawmen reached the Young America mine, and Al Cunningham veered off the road, heading for the buildings. Packard and Murdock rode on another two hundred yards to the Winnemucca mine. A few miners were milling about, carrying grease buckets and tools, and Packard and Murdock guided their mounts around the workers to haul up near the door of the main office.

As they dismounted, a skinny miner with a long beard came out the door. Smiling at Packard, he said, "Howdy, Sheriff."

"Howdy," Packard echoed. "Mr. Uzelac in?"

"Yep." Squinting at the lawman, the man inquired, "Trouble of some kind?"

"You might say that," Packard muttered, stepping past the miner and opening the door. Murdock followed him inside.

A portly, middle-aged woman sitting at a small desk near the door looked up at their entry. The sheriff gazed at the door of the mine owner's private office, which was at the rear, then said amiably, "Afternoon, Mrs. Uzelac. Is your husband in?"

Rising to her feet, Hannah Uzelac smiled and replied, "Yes, he is, Sheriff. I'll tell him you're here."

Packard thanked her and waited while she entered the rear office. Seconds later she emerged and said, "Go right on in, Sheriff."

When the lawmen stepped through the doorway, Art Uzelac was on his feet behind his big oak desk. A large black cigar stuck out one side of his mouth, and the room was filled with smoke.

The owner of the Winnemucca mine was more portly than his wife and bald except for a slight fringe of hair circling his head. His moon-shaped face was prone to redness, and his small, closely set eyes all but disappeared when he frowned or smiled. He was smiling now at the lawmen, and his eyes were barely visible. "Good afternoon, gentlemen," he said warmly. "Is this a social call or business?"

"I'm afraid it's business, Art—and unpleasant business at that," Packard responded.

"Oh?" Uzelac's bushy eyebrows arched.

"Cabel McKay just came in off his run from Sacramento, and his stage was bearing Webster Kirgan's body on the rack. Web had about a dozen slugs in him."

"Web . . . Web Kirgan is dead?" Uzelac took the cigar from his mouth and laid it in an ashtray on top of his desk. He coughed slightly, then said, "As you well know, I had no love for the man, but I sure wouldn't wish *that* on him. How and where did it happen?"

Packard related the story to him. "I've got to ask you a question, Art," he stated when he had finished.

Uzelac's plump face darkened. His eyes turned to pinpoints as he frowned and muttered, "I know what it's gonna be, but you're barkin' up the wrong tree, Sheriff. I didn't have anything to do with it."

"It's no secret you brought in six tough guys a couple of weeks ago, Art. I want to know—"

"They didn't do it!" snapped the mineowner, cutting off the sheriff. "I hired those men strictly as a defensive measure in this dispute between the Winnemucca and the Young America, not an offensive one. They're here to protect the miners of the Winnemucca, my staff, and me. I didn't hire them to come in here and start a war."

"Maybe they did it without your knowledge," suggested Ed Murdock.

"No!" blurted Uzelac. "The men I hire follow my orders . . . and I didn't order anybody to kill Kirgan!"

Packard shoved his hat back on his head. "Well, I'm going to have McKay and his shotgunner take a look at your new men and their horses, Art." Turning to his deputy, he said, "Ed, go get Cabel and Robby. If they're not at the hotel, they'll be at the Stockade Saloon."

Murdock wheeled and disappeared.

Uzelac picked up his cigar, stuck it in his mouth, and blustered, "Jess, this is an outrage! I take this as a personal insult!"

Keeping his temper, Packard replied, "I'm just doing my job, Art. If it were *your* body riddled full of bullets, where do you think I would have gone first?"

The portly man dabbed at his sweat-beaded brow. He grunted, admitting, "You'd have gone to see Troop."

"Precisely. You two have had everything but a war going on for months. I was afraid something like this was going to happen."

Uzelac blew a smoke ring toward the ceiling. "Well, you can believe what you want, but none of my bunch had anything to do with killing Kirgan."

"Then you won't mind if McKay and Lyons take a look at your new men," the sheriff rejoined. "Look, since Ed will be back here with them shortly, why don't you go assemble your men out front?"

When the stage driver and his partner arrived, they stood beside Sheriff Jess Packard, scrutinizing Art Uzelac's six new men and their horses. The mineowner stood next to his men with a petulant look on his beefy face. Packard let Cabel McKay and Robby Lyons study the motley-looking group of men for several minutes, then asked, "Well, what do you say?"

The driver and shotgunner looked at each other, then shook their heads. "These ain't the men who stopped the stage and murdered Web Kirgan," McKay replied. "Not a stitch of clothing, a hat, a boot, a saddle, or a horse is familiar."

"You're absolutely sure?"

"Absolutely," McKay affirmed.

"That's right, Sheriff," Lyons concurred. "These men didn't do it."

"Now, just a minute," Ed Murdock interjected. "What if the three men who killed Kirgan are here but had different horses, equipment, and clothing? They could have switched, you know."

Lyons shook his head. "Still wouldn't change anything. All three men who stopped the stage were tall and skinny. There isn't a man in this bunch who's that skinny or that tall. Right, Cabel?"

"That's keerect," McKay answered.

Uzelac took a deep breath and sighed. "Well, Jess, does that satisfy you?"

Rubbing his chin, the sheriff replied, "Yeah, it does."

A victorious expression spread over Uzelac's face. "Then I expect an apology. You've taken up a good deal of my valuable time and deterred these men from doing their duties."

Packard's jaw jutted stubbornly. "I don't apologize either for taking up your time or for deterring these men. I wouldn't have been doing my job if I hadn't checked your men out. But I do apologize for thinking that you had ordered Web killed."

The mineowner nodded. "Apology accepted."

The driver and shotgunner headed back to town, and Packard and Murdock rode to the Young America mine. While covering the short distance that separated the mines, the sheriff mused aloud, "Who else would want Web Kirgan dead?"

"Beats the tar out of me, boss," replied Murdock. "Maybe it's somebody with a personal grudge that has nothing to do with this mine squabble."

"Could be," Packard said. "Well, let's see how Al's doing with Mr. Troop."

Looking in the direction of the Young America mine office, they saw a tight knot of men gathered in front and heard a sharp voice filling the air. As they drew closer, they recognized it as Virgil Troop's.

When they veered off the road and headed for the cluster of buildings and people, the tall, slender Troop spotted them and elbowed his way through the press. His face beet red, he boomed as Packard drew up, "Sheriff, did you make an arrest?"

Dismounting, Packard shook his head and answered, "No, Virgil, I didn't."

"Well, why not? Uzelac and his bunch killed Web as sure as I'm standing here talking to you!"

"You're wrong about that," the sheriff replied levelly. Explaining that the new men were built nothing like the killers, Packard concluded, "I'm sorry, but Web's murderers have still not been found."

As the visibly angry Troop drew closer, his slight limp—due to a mining accident several years before—seemed more pronounced. His pale-eyed stare clung steadily to Packard's face as he hissed, "Well, you're the law around here! Track those killers down and bring 'em to justice!"

Packard responded, "I'll do my best, Virgil, but this is a big country. Tracking down the killers could prove impossible."

"*Impossible?*" roared Troop. "What are you talking about? That badge on your chest says you have to catch 'em!"

"Even if I worked full-time with my deputies and a posse of a hundred men, there are thousands of places where they could hole up," Packard pointed out. "I'll do my best, but you've got to be reasonable about this."

Troop said nothing for a long moment. Finally he met the sheriff's own penetrating gaze and responded, "I don't like this one bit, Jess, but go see what you can do."

Watching the lawmen as they mounted up and rode away, the mineowner stood silently, though it was evident that he was infuriated. When Packard and Murdock were out of sight, Troop turned to his men and declared heatedly, "I don't care what that stage crew says, I know it was Uzelac's men who killed Web! Now we're gonna fight fire with fire! I'm gonna hire some strong arms of my own!"

"You have some guys in mind, boss?" asked one of the men.

"I sure do," Troop growled. "Judd Colden and his men. I learned a couple of days ago that he and his gang are operating over in San Andreas, California."

The miners stood in awe, for Colden was known to be a cold-blooded cutthroat. One man asked, "Boss, would Colden stop whatever he's doin' and come to work for you?"

"We're pullin' a lot of gold outta this mine," Troop answered. "I assure you, the offer I'm gonna make Colden will bring him over the mountains. I'll write him a letter and send Curt out with it at dawn."

Twenty-year-old Curt Sibley was Troop's usual messenger. Young Sibley's life had been saved by Troop some four years previously when the youth and his family had been attacked by Paiute Indians. The rest of the family was killed, but the appearance of Troop and a number of his men had saved the teenager's life. Sibley had lived with Troop and worked for him ever since.

That evening Virgil Troop wrote a letter to Colden, explaining the trouble he was having with the Winnemucca

mine operators and saying Colden's presence would
guarantee no further trouble. He made the gang leader
a generous offer to bring five men and work for him,
pointing out that a group larger than six would look like
too much force in the eyes of the law.

Finishing the letter, Troop called Curt Sibley into
the room and handed him the sealed envelope. Ap-
praising the skinny, red-haired youth, the mineowner
told him, "Now, Curt, I want you to find Colden and
give him this envelope personally. Don't give it to
anyone else. Understand?"

"Yes, sir," Sibley assured him.

"Once you've put the envelope in his hand, wait
right there till he reads it. The letter tells him to give
you his answer. If it's yes—which I'm sure it will be—
have him also tell you when he and his men will get
here. Ride back as fast as you can."

"I will, sir," Sibley promised.

"Good. Oh, and Curt, do you remember the way
station at the top of Sonora Pass."

"Yes, sir."

"A man named McGuire runs it." Pulling a couple of
gold pieces from his pocket, Troop dropped them in the
messenger's palm and said, "Here's some money. Since
your own animal will be worn out if you ride hard up
the pass, rent one of McGuire's spare horses to give
you a fresh mount to ride down the other side of the
pass. You can pick up your own horse on the way back."

Sibley nodded. "I'll do everything exactly as you
want."

It was high noon when Curt Sibley rode his lathered,
puffing horse up to the McGuire Way Station at the
crest of the 9,628-foot Sonora Pass. The air was thin and
quite cool at that altitude, and though the road was dry,

there were patches of icy snow in the shady spots beneath the large pine trees that dotted the mountains. Large boulders and rocks, most of which were still embedded in the snow, lay scattered amid the trees, waiting to trip up an unwary traveler foolish enough to stray from the road.

Two wagons were parked near the porch of the main building, and several saddle horses were tied to the hitch rail nearby as Sibley dismounted. After walking his mount around for a few minutes to cool him down, he patted the animal's neck and told him, "You'll get a rest now, boy."

The youth stepped onto the porch of the large log building just as the door opened. A man, his wife, and three children came out, all carrying sacks of supplies, and headed for one of the wagons.

Entering the building, Sibley strode to the counter at the near end of the large room, where Everett McGuire was helping a customer load boxes with groceries from the well-stocked shelves. A huge stone fireplace with a blazing fire was at the far end of the room, and between the shelves and the fireplace was a door that led to the kitchen. Several comfortable chairs were arrayed in front of the fireplace, and in the middle of the floor were tables that served as the restaurant area, where three men were eating. Opposite the counter, some forty feet away, was the bar, where a half-dozen men stood drinking. One man was talking quite loud, boasting that he was a gunfighter and had put seventeen men in their graves.

As Sibley approached the counter, waiting for McGuire to finish with his customer, a beautiful young woman with shiny auburn hair came from the kitchen. Walking over to the youth, she asked, "May I help you?"

He was so captivated with her stunning beauty that it took him a few seconds to find his tongue. "Uh . . .

uh . . . er, yes," he finally stammered. "I need to leave my horse and rent one of yours. I just rode in from Aurora, and I'm headed for California. I'll be back tomorrow to pick up my animal."

Flashing a warm smile, the young woman said, "My uncle will have to help you with that."

McGuire had apparently overheard their conversation, for he paused in his work and looked at Sibley, saying, "I'll be with you in just a moment, young fella."

Absently nodding, the youth watched the young woman as she moved about the large room, straightening chairs and tidying up. One of the men at the bar tried to strike up a conversation with her, but she ignored the half-drunk traveler.

Everett McGuire helped the customer carry his goods outside to his wagon, then returned to take care of Sibley. Following Sibley's gaze, he smiled and remarked, "Gorgeous, isn't she?"

"That's putting it mildly," Sibley rejoined, lifting his hat and running splayed fingers through his carrot-red hair. "I've been in here a few times, Mr. McGuire, but I haven't seen her before."

"Angie just recently came to live with my wife and me. She's my younger brother's daughter, but both her parents are dead. She was living in Denver until—well, let's just say she decided a change of scenery would do her good. We invited her here so she'd have a place to live and could be with those who love her." McGuire did not confide that twenty-five-year-old Angie McGuire was nursing a broken heart, having been jilted by her fiancé so he could marry a rich woman.

Smiling at her uncle, Angie came behind the counter as McGuire asked Sibley, "Do you want to use your own saddle and bridle on my horse?"

"Yes, sir. And if all goes well, I'll be back here about this time tomorrow."

At that moment the gunslinger at the bar said something that he apparently thought was funny, and the rest of the men were forcing themselves to laugh. It was obvious that they were afraid of him.

Turning slightly so he could see the gunfighter, Sibley inquired, "Who is he, Mr. McGuire?"

"Hank Wesson. Ever hear of him?"

"I'll say!" the youth replied. Wesson had a dangerous reputation, and his name was spoken with a touch of fear. "That's Hank Wesson?"

"Yep. The two guys standing beside him are his cronies. Both of them are gunfighters, too. The one in the black hat is Slim Dyer. The other one is Gabe Hall."

Suddenly Wesson stepped away from the bar, waving a whiskey bottle. Looking at the few men who were seated at nearby tables, he boasted with a slurred tongue, "I'm goin' down to Aurora next, 'cause there's a man there that I'm just itchin' to brace. You fellas probably know him, 'cause he's sheriff there. Name's Jess Packard. He killed my best friend a month ago, so he's gonna die for that."

The men at the tables merely exchanged glances and shook their heads.

Gesturing for Sibley to follow him, McGuire crossed the room, heading for the front door. As he did so, he called to the drunken gunfighter, "Best thing for you to do, Mr. Wesson, is forget such a notion. Nobody can outdraw Jess Packard."

Wesson took a swig of whiskey and snorted. "Hah! Every man who lives by the gun eventually meets up with the man who's faster'n him. You're lookin' at the man who's gonna outdraw Packard."

Young Sibley stepped close to the gunslinger and advised, "I live in Aurora, Mr. Wesson, and I've seen Sheriff Packard in action. Believe me, you don't want to go against him." After a pause, he asked, "Was your friend a gunfighter?"

"Yeah. Roy Ambers."

Nodding slowly, Sibley remarked, "Oh, yeah. I was on the street when he challenged Sheriff Packard. The sheriff tried to talk Ambers out of drawing against him, but your friend was cocksure he could take him. He never even got his gun out of his holster."

"I ain't Ambers, kid," the gunfighter growled, shaking the whiskey bottle at him. "I'm Hank Wesson. I'm the man who's gonna put Packard six feet under, 'cause there ain't nobody faster'n me!"

Shrugging, McGuire mumbled, "Come on, Curt. What Mr. Wesson does is his business. Mine is getting you that horse you want." As the two of them headed out the door, the youth gave Angie McGuire one more admiring glance.

When McGuire returned alone a few minutes later, Angie helped him restock some shelves. While they were working, she asked, "Uncle Ev, have you met this Sheriff Jess Packard?"

"Sure have, honey," he replied. "He takes a trip over the pass every now and then and always stops in for a friendly chat. He's a right-fine fella. Handsome, too."

Looking thoughtful, Angie remarked, "I vaguely recall reading a story about his exploits in one of Denver's newspapers once. I can't remember the details, but I remember that the article said he's one of the most famous lawmen in the West."

"That's correct, honey," McGuire concurred. His voice filled with admiration, he added, "Jess Packard is the kind of lawman every town and every county needs, 'cause he takes a tough, no-nonsense approach with lawbreakers and troublemakers. When you're in his territory, you walk straight or pay the consequences."

*   *   *

In the Sierra foothills due east of San Andreas, California, gang leader Judd Colden and five of his men were crouched low behind a thicket in a shallow ravine, setting a gun trap for San Andreas town marshal Ted Wiley and his deputy, Alan Fox. Hard and tough, the tall, dark-complected Colden had a cruel set to his jaw and a cold look in his hazel eyes. Adding to his menacing mien was a jagged scar that ran from his left temple down to his upper lip and the straight black hair that hung long over his collar.

Regarding three of his rough, mean-looking men, Colden said, "You fellas haven't been with me when I've set up a gun trap before, so here's the plan: You'll head across the path and get down in those bushes, while Vince and Jocko'll stay here with me. Stay low and out of sight till I fire the first shot. That'll be your signal to empty both guns into those rotten badge-toters while the three of us get 'em from this side."

Obeying their leader, Mel Blanford, Gene Ortiz, and George Locke—each holding revolvers in both of their hands—hurried across the forest ravine and ducked into the brush on the opposite side of the path.

Vince Denning, a callous killer and Colden's right-hand man, was short, thick-bodied, and had a cake of ice for a heart. Massive Jocko Bane, Colden's personal bodyguard, stood well over six feet and weighed three hundred pounds—all of it muscle. His repulsive face was a clear indication of his savagery; in a fight he delighted in leaving an opponent lying in a bloody heap, an inch from death.

Colden was gleaning a merciless satisfaction from setting up this gun trap, knowing it was a sure way of killing the lawmen. While the sun climbed in the California sky, the bandit thought of how Wiley had come close to squelching the shady deals Colden had been pulling in San Andreas with the intent of one day controlling the town and its wealth. Learning that Wiley had caught on to him and was assembling proof that would send Colden and his cohorts to prison, the outlaw decided it was time for Wiley to die.

Things fell conveniently into place earlier that morning when the marshal and his deputy had been called out of town to settle a problem between two ranchers. Colden and his men had followed, observing the lawmen from a distance, and when Wiley and Fox had been about to return to town, the outlaws had hurried ahead and positioned themselves strategically, prepared to open fire when the lawmen were in the most vulnerable spot in the ravine.

Suddenly Denning touched Colden's arm and whispered, "Here they come!"

Looking across the path to the bushes that hid his other men, Colden hissed, "Get ready! Here they come!"

Moments later Wiley and Fox came riding into the ravine and ironically were discussing their plan to catch Judd Colden in his crooked ways and see that he and his gang went to prison. Overhearing them, Colden smiled to himself, knowing the plan would never be realized. He raised both revolvers and waited impatiently as the unsuspecting lawmen rode closer to the trap. Seconds passed, and then Wiley and Fox were in the perfect spot. Colden's guns boomed, and suddenly the ravine rocked with gunfire.

Bullets ripped into the pair from both sides, knocking them from their saddles, and their terrified horses galloped away. When the twelve revolvers had been emptied, the outlaws came out of the brush and stood over their victims. The marshal and his deputy lay sprawled on the path, riddled with bullets.

Laughing triumphantly, Colden announced, "Well, the world now has two fewer badge-toters and is better off for it! Let's go."

*   *   *

A short time later, the gang hauled up in front of their cabin just outside of San Andreas and dismounted. "Let's open a bottle of whiskey and celebrate, boys," Judd Colden suggested, and he and his men settled into the chairs ringing the large kitchen table.

As his men filled their shot glasses, Colden grinned and stated, "As soon as Reedy and the others get back from their trip to Nevada, we'll start the wheels rollin'. We'll need full manpower to make it happen, but soon we'll own San Andreas!"

Chapter Three

Aurora's Pine Street was showing signs of life early the next morning as stores and shops began to open their doors, but it was still relatively quiet.

Hugo Stern, a husky miner employed at the Young America, was standing on the boardwalk in front of the Lonesome Pine Saloon, waiting for its seven-thirty opening. Armed with a revolver on his hip and a large hunting knife in a sheath on his belt, Stern was feeling the need for a good stiff drink before reporting to work at the mine, for the murdered Web Kirgan had been a real friend to him.

Shifting impatiently from one foot to the other, Stern looked up at the sound of heavy boots on the boardwalk and saw Marvin Eggars walking toward him. The burly Eggars was a miner at the Winnemucca, and feeling contempt for anyone connected with Art Uzelac, Stern filled his mouth with saliva as the other miner drew near.

Other than glancing quickly at Stern, Eggars ignored him. He was about to pass Stern when the Young America man spat a stream directly in front of him, striking the boardwalk and splattering Eggars's boots. Halting, Eggars narrowed his eyes and growled, "Were you aimin' at my boots?"

"Nope," came the curt reply. "But what if I was?"

His face reddening with anger, the unarmed Eggars

warned, "I'd stuff that dirty hat of yours down your throat, that's what."

"You and what army?" challenged Stern.

"If you got a beef, let's hear it," Eggars snapped.

"I got a beef, all right! That snake you work for sent his hired killers out to murder my boss!"

Eggars bristled. His countenance hardened as he retorted, "That's a rotten lie! Sheriff Packard found that possibility to have no foundation. I don't know who killed Web Kirgan, but it wasn't anybody from the Winnemucca."

"Who else would want Web dead?" Stern railed.

"Maybe it was somebody in your own outfit that had a grudge to satisfy!" Eggars snarled.

The argument was getting hotter and louder when Deputy Al Cunningham arrived on the scene and stepped into the fray. Pushing his way past the growing number of onlookers, Cunningham blared, "Hey, you two! Break it up!"

Hugo Stern turned halfway around to see who was barking the command. Scowling, he spat, "Get outta here and mind your own business, Cunningham!"

"Watch your mouth, Stern!" retorted the deputy. "This kind of stuff *is* my business."

"Bah! You oughta be over at the Winnemucca arrestin' the dirty skunks who murdered my boss! *That's* supposed to be your business!"

"You know full well that the sheriff has established that Kirgan's murderers aren't connected with the Winnemucca!" Cunningham declared.

Stern laughed humorlessly, swore, and rasped, "Yeah, for a price."

Cunningham was visibly bristled. "What do you mean by that?" he demanded.

"You know what I mean. Wouldn't you look the other

way if Art Uzelac stuffed your hands full of gold under the table?"

The deputy abruptly took hold of Stern's arm and ordered, "Okay, you're coming with me to repeat that low-down accusation directly to the sheriff!"

Stern stiffened and planted his feet. "I ain't gonna talk to that hypocrite lawman!"

Cunningham tightened his grip. "Oh, yes, you are!"

Stern's hand moved in a flash, drawing the long-bladed knife from its sheath and plunging it into Cunningham's chest. The deputy grunted, grasping the haft, and fell.

Horrified gasps rose from the onlookers, who seemed too shocked to react. Swearing, Marvin Eggars jumped on Stern's back, and the two men slammed into the front of the saloon, then crashed to the boardwalk. Eggars swung a fist at Stern but missed, and Stern chopped him hard, dazing him. While the stunned crowd looked on, the miner pulled his gun, cocked it, and fired directly into Eggars's face.

The bystanders started screaming and shouting. One man wheeled and began running down the street, calling the sheriff's name, but Stern drew a bead on him and fired. The man arched his back and fell.

Pointing his gun at the bystanders, most of whom were unarmed, Stern snarled ferociously, "Get outta my way!"

A path quickly cleared, and he bolted for a horse tied to the hitch rail across the street. Loosening the reins, he leapt into the saddle and galloped out of town, heading east toward the desert.

Having heard the gunshot from his office nearly two blocks away, Sheriff Jess Packard came racing up the street. A babel of voices assaulted the sheriff's ears as he arrived and found Marvin Eggars and the bystander dead. Kneeling beside Cunningham, he determined that the deputy was alive but barely conscious. He asked a couple of the onlookers to go summon the other deputies while he and several other men carried Cunningham to Dr. Jacob Wren's office. As they walked, one of the bearers told him what happened.

Soon after the doctor had examined Cunningham and solemnly told Packard that the deputy was critical and could die, Neil Thurston, Ed Murdock, and Lee Austin arrived. The enraged Packard took his other deputies outside and told them, "I'm going after Stern. You keep an eye on the town."

"You shouldn't go alone, boss," Austin remarked. "Let me go with you."

"I can handle it," the sheriff countered. "Don't worry, when I catch him I won't kill him—much as I'd like to. But there's liable to be more of this kind of trouble, and I need you here."

With that, Jess Packard dashed down the street to his horse and rode out of town in pursuit. Lashing the animal and digging his spurs deep into its flanks, he pushed it for all the speed it could give. Within twenty minutes, he caught sight of a small dust cloud a couple of miles ahead, and soon he was close enough to identify Hugo Stern's bulky form in the saddle. The gallant beast beneath Packard was steadily closing the gap between them.

Bounding over the rolling desert, Stern pushed his stolen horse hard, but after a while the animal became winded. When barely a hundred yards remained between the hunter and the hunted, the killer glanced back over his shoulder at Packard. Stern whipped out his gun and fired at his pursuer, but the bullet chewed dirt far off target. Cursing loudly, Stern fired again, but Packard knew that the chances of accuracy when firing a pistol from the back of a galloping horse were next to nil. Blinking against the wind caused by the fast speed, the lawman pressed on.

Stern stubbornly kept firing until his revolver was empty. Holstering the weapon, he gouged the animal's sides, but it was to no avail. The sheriff was now pulling alongside.

In a final effort, Stern pulled the revolver and threw it at Packard, but the lawman ducked it, then jumped from his saddle. His strong fingers sank into the miner's thick shoulders, and they were airborne together for a few seconds before hitting the ground hard, plowing into the sand.

Packard was on his feet first. He could have drawn his weapon, held Stern at gunpoint, and taken him back to town immediately, but the wrath he felt for what the man had done to his deputy was screaming for release. When Stern clambered to his feet, Packard slugged him square on the jaw. The miner went down hard, and Packard stood over him, ready to dish out more.

While Stern lay on his back, rolling his head in pain, the lawman blared, "Why did you stab my deputy, you rotten scum? Why did you stab my deputy?"

Suddenly Stern stiffened and kicked Packard's feet out from under him. When the sheriff hit the ground, the miner went for Packard's holstered gun. He had it partly out when the sheriff seized him by the shirtcollar and, shifting his weight, brought the miner down, savagely slamming his face into the ground.

Stern grunted and struggled to bring his head up, but Packard's arms were like steel bands. He banged the man's face into the hard ground repeatedly until Stern turned rubbery and collapsed, unconscious. His breath sawing in and out of him, Packard grabbed a pair of handcuffs from his saddlebag and shackled the miner's hands. That done, Packard hauled him up and hoisted him onto the back of the stolen horse.

Hugo Stern's nose was broken, and his face was caked with blood. Coming to, the husky miner sat hunched over in the saddle, spitting blood and several broken teeth. When Packard took the reins of Stern's horse and swung into his own saddle, the battered miner lifted his head slightly and looked at him. Blood dribbled down his chin as he mumbled, "What are you gonna do with me?"

"That's a stupid question," the sheriff grated. "I'm taking you to jail to face murder charges for killing two men. If Al Cunningham dies, it'll be three. Your next stop will be at the end of a rope."

Outlaws Bob Reedy, Lloyd Hice, Wes Ardahl, and Franklin Kreeger rode at a steady pace across the Nevada desert, heading west toward Sonora Pass and eager to rejoin the rest of the Colden gang at San Andreas.

The desert floor was pocked with gulches and arroyos, and toward midmorning the riders topped a sandy rise and caught sight of two Paiute Indians on horseback, dipping into an arroyo. Knowing his men hated Indians as much as he did, Reedy raised a hand and pulled rein. "Did you see what I saw?" he asked, grinning evilly.

"Yeah," Kreeger replied with a chuckle. "A couple of insects with red skin just rode into that gully."

"What say we corner 'em and rid the world of them pesky insects?"

"We'd better not shoot 'em," advised Kreeger. "They might have buddies close by."

"Good thinkin'. We'll disarm 'em, then kill 'em with our knives," Reedy stated. "Come on."

Paiute chieftain Joaquin Jim and his friend Tontaya were in conversation as they rode side by side in the arroyo. Their appearance was quite similar, as both were dressed in buckskins and wore sidearms, and their shoulder-length black hair sported bright red headbands.

The Indians found themselves surrounded by four white men charging over the sides of the arroyo, their rifle muzzles aimed at them. The white men's eyes were gleaming wickedly.

The Indians pulled rein as Bob Reedy drew up in front of them and barked, "Get your hands in the air, scum!"

"What do you want?" asked Joaquin Jim, obeying the command.

"I want you off those animals," Reedy shouted. "Fast!"

The chieftain and his partner looked at each other fearfully and slid to the ground. While Reedy held his gun on them, the other outlaws dismounted and took the Paiutes' sidearms.

Lloyd Hice laughed gleefully, saying, "We got 'em, Bob! By dingies, we got 'em! Are we ever gonna have fun now!"

As it was obvious that Reedy was in charge, Joaquin Jim looked him square in the eye, repeating, "What do you want?"

Reedy slid from his saddle and stepped close to the Paiute. Gritting his teeth, he replied, "I want you dead, red scum. That's what I want."

A shadow seemed to scuttle across Joaquin Jim's eyes. His face grim, he said in a deep basso, "You would be a fool to kill us, white man. Our village is close by. My braves will cut you to pieces. I am their chief."

Reedy snickered and trembled mockingly. "Gee, I'm shakin' all over! Let's face it, if your village was all that close, you'd be hollerin' your head off for help."

Turning to his friends, he said, "Let's take 'em back to that stand of junipers we passed a little ways back and tie 'em to the trees. Then we'll have our fun. We'll gag 'em so's they can't holler while we torture 'em." He sneered, adding, "We'll show 'em what real pain is, then when we've had enough fun, we'll kill 'em by cuttin' 'em to pieces like so much rotten meat!'"

Held at gunpoint, the Indians were bound and gagged, then led to the trees. Cold sweat beaded the Paiutes' faces as they were lashed to the junipers, facing each other. Suddenly a loud voice cut the warm desert air. "Hold it right there!"

The outlaws spun around to see Sheriff Jess Packard astride his horse, holding his cocked Colt .45 on them. On horseback behind him was his bound prisoner.

Joaquin Jim and Tontaya looked at each other with relief. They were well acquainted with Packard, for it was he who had negotiated the truce with the chieftain the year before.

Packard's voice was filled with anger as he rode closer and demanded, "What's going on here?"

Noting by Packard's badge that he was the sheriff of Esmeralda County, Reedy knew he and his cronies were dealing with the man regarded as the toughest lawman west of the Rockies. After glancing at his friends, the outlaw looked at Packard and, laughing hollowly, answered, "Nothin' serious, Sheriff. We . . . uh . . . we were just havin' a little fun. We weren't gonna hurt 'em or nothin'.'"

"Untie them and take those gags out of their mouths, and then give them back their guns!"

While the order was being carried out, Packard asked the Indian chieftain, "Joaquin Jim, what's this all about?"

The Paiute described what had happened—including how the white men had said they were going to torture and kill them.

Packard's voice was menacing as he looked at Reedy and asked, "Just having a little fun, huh?"

Reedy's face blanched. "Now, wait a minute, Sheriff! That was all just a joke! We weren't really gonna torture or kill 'em. Honest! We were just gonna scare 'em good, then let 'em go."

"You stupid fools!" the lawman declared scathingly. "Up until a year ago, the Paiutes, Monaches, and Mojaves were attacking and killing white people all over these parts. Your 'little fun' could once again start the Indians on the warpath! Seems to me the best place for the likes of you four is behind bars."

Reedy threw up his hands and yelped, "Wait a minute! Like I told you, we was only funnin'! Okay, maybe we were bein' stupid, but we're sorry. Right, fellas?"

His cohorts readily concurred.

Feeling certain that he had just saved Joaquin Jim and Tontaya from torture and death, Packard also knew that he could not actually prove it. All he could do was issue a stern warning and send the foursome on their way.

"Where are you men from?" he asked harshly.

"California," replied Reedy.

"The California border's about sixteen miles from here. How long do you think it would take you to get there?"

"We can do it in an hour, Sheriff," replied Reedy, his tone contrite.

"All right, I'm going to let you go. You get your carcasses over the border and keep on riding. If I see you around here again, I'm liable to have a change of heart and put you behind bars for endangering the lives of white people in Nevada. Go on. Git!"

Clearly relieved to get off easily, the outlaws mounted up and galloped away in a cloud of dust. When they were out of sight, Packard turned to the chieftain and said, "Joaquin Jim, I'm truly sorry about this. I hope what those men did won't cause you to go on the warpath."

The Paiute smiled. "The act of four brainless white

fools will not cause me to break our truce, Sheriff Packard. But I am certain that those men were indeed going to torture and kill us. We are grateful to you for saving our lives." Shaking hands Indian-style with Packard, the Paiutes mounted and rode away.

The lawman swung into his saddle and continued with his prisoner back to Aurora. Arriving in town, he went directly to his office where his three deputies were standing at the door, talking to several men. Seeing the sheriff approaching, Lee Austin disengaged himself from the others and stepped up to the hitch rail as Packard reined in.

Austin's face was filled with grief as he said, "Sheriff, I've got bad news. Al didn't make it. He died about a half hour ago."

His dread over Al Cunningham's fate confirmed, Packard grew even more furious. He nodded stiffly to Austin, dismounted, and stepped to Stern's horse. Glaring at the prisoner, he rasped, "It'll give me the greatest pleasure to watch you take the plunge at the end of a rope!"

Reaching up, he jerked the burly miner from the saddle, slamming him to the ground. It was apparent that Packard's temper was out of control, and Austin laid a firm hand on his boss's arm and said, "Sheriff, let's take Stern inside and lock him up."

Packard's entire body was quivering with rage, and his breathing was ragged. Realizing his deputy was attempting to prevent him from doing something he would regret later, he muttered, "Yeah. Let's lock him up before he gets hurt."

When Stern was shoved into the cell and the door was locked, Packard put his face close to the bars and growled, "I'm going to see that you get your trial as soon as possible, Stern. That way justice will be served all the sooner."

Taking his deputies into the office, Packard sat down at his desk and filled them in on Stern's capture. He was informing them of the incident with the Paiutes and the four white men from California when Virgil Troop's lanky figure appeared at the open door. Looking past his men, the lawman asked, "What can I do for you, Virgil?"

Limping into the office, the grim-faced mineowner replied, "I understand you've got Hugo Stern locked up."

"That's right," responded the sheriff, rising and moving around the desk.

"Before we talk about him, I want to know what you've done to track down the men who killed Web."

"Everything I could," Packard stated. "I went out to the spot where the stage was stopped, but the killers left no clues of any kind. I'm afraid I've reached a dead end. There's nothing else I can do."

Troop's face showed his skepticism, and he grunted, "Nothing else, huh?"

Perturbed by the man's attitude, Packard remarked, "If you've got any suggestions on what else I could do, I'm all ears."

Troop was silent for a long moment, then made a conciliatory gesture and said, "Actually, I came here to ask a favor about Hugo. He's been a good employee and has been real loyal to me—and to Web. From what I heard about the incident this morning, Hugo just let his emotions get away from him. I'm asking you to go easy on him and see if you can talk the judge into giving him life in prison rather than executing him."

Packard's dark brown eyes narrowed. Clipping each word, he stated, "I will make no such attempt. Stern deliberately killed three men this morning—including one of my deputies. The law will take its course, Virgil. Unless the men on the jury are out of their minds, they'll find Stern guilty of murder. And I'm sure the judge will want him to hang."

Troop left the office in a huff, and the sheriff sent his three deputies out to patrol the town. He then went to warn the two newspaper publishers to exercise caution when it came to writing about the feud between the Young America and Winnemucca mines. After talking to Brad Lafferty, the owner of the *Esmeralda Union,* he walked to the office of the *Aurora Times.*

Stepping inside, he waved to his younger brother, who was busy at the press, then strode over to Derek Wood's desk. Wood looked up and smiled, and Monica came out of her office and planted a kiss on Packard's cheek, saying, "We heard about Hugo Stern, darling. I'm glad you caught him. And I'm so sorry about Al."

"Me, too," Packard replied sadly. "He was one of the best." Turning to his future father-in-law, he said, "Sir, I just paid a visit to Brad Lafferty, and I need to tell you what I told him. Be real careful what you print about the mine feud. This town is sitting on a virtual powder keg—we saw evidence of that this morning—and the slightest spark could ignite it."

Holding on to his arm possessively, Monica nodded her agreement.

Wood replied, "I understand, Jess. You have my word that we won't print anything inflammatory."

"I appreciate it, sir. Thank you."

Monica squeezed Jess's arm and told him, "I stopped by our new house on the way to work this morning, darling. It's coming along fine."

"Good," Packard declared, grinning. "I've been so busy these past few days, I haven't had a chance to check on it. Are they on schedule?"

"Looks to me like they're ahead of schedule," she replied.

"Excellent. Well, I'd better be going."

"Jess," called Alex, crossing the room. "Before you go, there's something I need to tell you."

"What's that?" queried the sheriff.

"I was talking to one of Virgil Troop's miners this morning after you rode out in pursuit of Hugo Stern, and he told me that Virgil sent Curt Sibley to California to bring some men in to beef up their strength against Uzelac's bunch."

His face stiffening, Packard stated, "That means we're in for more trouble."

Monica peered into her fiancé's dark eyes. "Come with me. I know a way to put a smile on that worried face," she said coyly. Taking her man by the hand, she led him into her private office.

When the door was closed behind them, the lawman and the beautiful blonde shared a long, tender kiss. While he held her close, she whispered into his ear, "Our wedding day is getting closer, darling. Our new house will soon be finished, and we can start buying furniture. Oh, I'm so excited!"

They kissed again, but it was interrupted by a sharp voice from the street.

"Jess Packard! I know you're in there! Come on out!"

Chapter Four

Jess Packard felt Monica Wood's body stiffen at the sound of the harsh command from the street. Releasing her, he opened her office door and looked across the room through the open outer doorway. Two men stood within a few feet of each other, facing the newspaper office and wearing tied-down guns. One was slender and the other was rather stocky.

Peering over his shoulder, Monica asked in a shaky voice, "Who are they, Jess?"

The slender one was shouting his name again as the lawman replied, "I don't know, honey. I don't recognize either one of them. The one that's shooting off his mouth is probably another greenhorn fool wanting to prove he can outdraw me."

Gripping his arm, Monica pleaded, "Jess, be careful."

The blonde was a step behind him as Packard left her office and headed for the front door. Alex Packard and Derek Wood were looking out the front window, and Alex stepped beside his older brother and suggested, "Jess, there are two of them. I'll get my gun and even up the odds."

"No, stay inside," Packard countered, shaking his head emphatically. "I don't want you mixing in. Lola needs her husband, and my niece and nephew need their father. I'll handle it."

"Please, darling," interjected Monica. "Let Alex go

with you. Facing two men at the same time is too dangerous."

"It'll be all right. I know their kind. If they're looking to make names for themselves, they'll take me on one at a time. There's no glory in two men killing one man."

Stepping through the doorway onto the boardwalk, Packard eyed Slim Dyer coldly, then gave the same look to the stocky Gabe Hall. Looking back at Dyer, he asked, "Who are you, and what do you want?"

"My name isn't important," replied Dyer, "and it ain't me that wants you."

Packard's gaze shifted to Hall.

"It ain't him that wants you, either," Dyer stated. Pointing twenty yards up the street to a rugged-looking man in a quick-draw stance, he said, "That's the fella who wants you. Hank Wesson."

People were collecting on both sides of the street, and the sheriff caught a glimpse of his three deputies coming his way as he focused on the hard-bitten gunman who stood in the middle of the street under the harsh midday sun, staring at him. Wesson's name was well-known to the lawman, for he had carved his notch in the ranks of gunfighters.

Packard's face tensed as he stepped into the street and turned toward the somber-looking Wesson. Briefly glancing at Dyer, he remarked, "It seems a bit senseless for Wesson to come here to brace me. Killing me wouldn't help his reputation any."

"He ain't here to kill you for the sake of his reputation," responded Dyer. "Four weeks ago you gunned down a fella named Roy Ambers. He was Hank's best friend—and Hank's here to square it."

"I see," Packard muttered, shifting his gaze momentarily to his deputies, who were approaching their boss.

As the three lawmen drew up, Ed Murdock asked

quietly, "You want us to handle the situation and run these men out of town?"

Holding his hard gaze once again on Wesson, Packard replied, "They'd only come back. You see, Mr. Wesson there, has a burr under his saddle. Seems that Ambers fella I had to kill a few weeks ago was his best friend, and he wants to make me pay. If I can't talk him into giving it up, I'll have to take Mr. Wesson out."

Gabe Hall snickered, "You ain't fast enough to do that, tin star."

Still staring intently at Wesson, Packard rasped, "Don't bet on it, friend."

Packard started walking slowly toward the gunfighter, who stood with his feet slightly apart and his hands at his sides. His men stayed beside Packard, moving at the same pace, while Dyer and Hall were on their heels.

As Packard got closer to Wesson, the onlookers began deserting the street, taking refuge in the buildings on both sides. Even the benches on the hotel porch were vacated. The lawman assumed that his fellow citizens questioned whether he could take on a shooter as fast as Wesson and feared the possibility of stray bullets.

When the sheriff was within forty feet of Wesson, he halted. His deputies veered off onto the boardwalk, and the gunfighter's cronies moved to the other side of the street. Still in his quick-draw stance, Hank Wesson reached up with his left hand and pulled his hat brim a little lower, shading his eyes from the sun.

A menacing stillness, a sense of violence about to explode, pervaded Pine Street. The people watching intently from windows and doors had observed similar scenes many times in the last four years, for numerous men had ridden into Aurora, hoping to make a name for themselves by outdrawing the famous Jess Packard. All of them lay moldering in their graves at Boot Hill, just outside of town—but none of them had had Hank Wesson's reputation.

A gust of wind blew along the rutted street, throwing up dust, and somewhere in the residential section a dog began barking. When the barking died out on the breeze, Packard said coolly, "Your friend Roy Ambers made the same mistake you're making right now, Wesson."

"He wasn't in your league, and you knew it, Packard!" came the taut reply. "You didn't have to kill him."

"I tried to talk him out of it, but he went for his gun. I had no choice. And if you make the same stupid mistake, an hour from now you'll be buried beside him, and Aurora's undertaker will have made fifteen dollars for digging your grave."

Grinning sardonically, Wesson challenged, "Afraid, tin star? Is that why you're tryin' so hard to talk me out of drawin' against you?" As he spoke, the gunslinger's hand dipped for his revolver.

His own hand a blur of motion, Jess Packard drew his Colt .45, cocked it, and aimed it at Wesson's chest. His adversary froze with his own weapon only halfway out of the holster. "I don't want to kill you, mister," the sheriff stated. "Let go of the gun and you'll see the sunset; pull it, and the sun will set over your grave."

Wesson licked his dry lips. It was obvious that his mind was whirling with conflict: Pride no doubt told him to pull the gun anyway and die like the man he was supposed to be . . . but probably a clawing in his belly made him drop the revolver back in the holster as if it had suddenly turned red-hot.

Packard eased the hammer down on his gun and holstered it. Glaring at his adversary, he said, "You're through as a gunfighter, Wesson. Tuck your tail between your legs and get out of my town."

Wheeling around, the sheriff started back up the street. He had taken only a few steps when he heard a familiar scraping sound—that of a gun sliding from a holster. Wesson was going to shoot him in the back. The lawman pivoted at the same time that his three deputies called out a warning. As Packard spun around, pulling his gun, he dropped to the ground. Wesson's weapon fired first, the slug cutting the air where the sheriff had been a split second before and chewing into the tailgate of a wagon. While the report of Wesson's gun was still echoing, Packard fired his Colt .45—and his aim was deadly accurate.

Even while Wesson was falling, the life gone from his body from the bullet exploding in his heart, Slim Dyer and Gabe Hall were reaching for their guns to kill Packard. But the three deputies whipped out their weapons, and for a few seconds Pine Street sounded like a battlefield as Hank Wesson's cronies were cut down in a hail of hot lead.

The gun smoke was still hanging in the air when the street was suddenly filled with people dashing out of the stores and shops, patting Packard on the back and congratulating him. Monica pushed her way through the crowd that encircled her fiancé and wrapped her arms around him, saying, "Jess, darling, there is no lawman in the West who can match you for courage and speed with his gun! I'm so proud that I'll soon be the wife of the best man who ever wore a badge!"

Grinning modestly, the sheriff protested, "That might be stretching it a little, honey. A lot of men much better than me have worn badges."

Monica shook her head and, her face filled with pride, retorted, "Nonsense, darling! You mark my word. One day you'll be written up in the history books as the West's number-one lawman, and it'll be an honor for me to be known as Mrs. Jess Packard!"

* * *

At San Andreas, Judd Colden sat at the table in the cabin, absently running his finger along his scar. Playing cards were fanned in his left hand, and a pile of gold double eagles sat in the middle of the table. The game was five-card stud, and the others at the table were Vince Denning, Mel Blanford, and Gene Ortiz. A whiskey bottle sat near Colden's elbow, and each man had a shot glass in front of him. A slight breeze blew through the cabin, and the late-afternoon sun threw shafts of light through the windows on the west side.

Draped like a massive rag doll on a nearby stuffed chair, Jocko Bane chuckled and said, "Sure feels good, don't it, Judd?"

Colden was concentrating on the cards he was holding. A few seconds passed before he mumbled, "What say, Jocko?"

"I said, don't it feel good?"

"Don't what feel good?"

"Knowin' Marshal Wiley and his deputy are out of the way."

"Oh, that. Yeah. You bet it feels good. As soon as the townspeople find their bodies, we'll muscle our way in. I hope Bob and the others get back soon. I want him to take over as town marshal."

"It's gonna be fun, ownin' us a town," put in George Locke. "I ain't never owned part of a town before."

"Stick with me, my friend," Colden said with a laugh. "Maybe one day we'll own us a whole county."

The men's victorious laughter ended abruptly at the sound of rumbling hooves. George Locke sprang to his feet and dashed to the window, peered out, then exclaimed, "It's Bob and the boys!"

Bob Reedy, Lloyd Hice, Wes Ardahl, and Franklin Kreeger thundered into the small yard in a cloud of dust, and Colden and the others filed outside as they dismounted.

"Glad to see you back, Bob," Colden said. "Got some good news for you."

"I can always use that," responded Reedy, stepping onto the porch. "Let's hear it."

"Come on inside and we'll talk about it over a glass of whiskey."

Filled in on what had transpired, Reedy and the men who had ridden with him were elated to learn that the gun trap set for Marshal Ted Wiley and his deputy had been successful. Colden then explained his plan to slowly gain control of San Andreas, and easing back in his chair and sipping at his whiskey, he remarked, "Here's the part you'll like best, Bob: I'm gonna install you as marshal. How does that strike you?"

"Rings my bell just fine, boss," Reedy quipped. "I've always thought I'd look good with a shiny badge on my chest."

Looking at Kreeger, Colden told him, "Franklin, you'll be Bob's deputy."

A sly grin worked its way over Kreeger's evil mouth. "Sounds good to me, boss. With Bob and me runnin' the marshal's office, we can make things go just like we want 'em. We're all gonna get rich."

Colden downed the rest of the whiskey in his glass, thumped the glass on the table, and chuckled. "That's exactly right. I'm gonna be like a king on a throne, overseein' my kingdom. Three months from now, we'll change San Andreas's name to Coldenville."

There was a burst of laughter, then Reedy's face became stony. "Unfortunately, some plans of our own didn't come to pass."

"Whaddya mean?" queried the dark-skinned outlaw.

Reedy explained about coming upon the two Paiute Indians and how their plans to torture and kill them were foiled by Sheriff Jess Packard. He finished his tale by quoting Packard's warning never to show up in Esmeralda County again.

Colden was about to comment when George Locke called from across the room, "We got company, boss. A rider's approachin' the cabin."

The outlaws turned their attention to the youthful rider as he hauled up to the porch. Colden and Locke stepped outside, eyeing him suspiciously, while the rider remained in the saddle and said, "I was told in town that I could find Mr. Judd Colden here."

"I'm Colden," acknowledged the gang leader.

"My name is Curt Sibley, sir. I was sent here by Virgil Troop, owner of the Young America mine in Aurora, Nevada."

"I've heard of the mine, kid," Colden allowed. "What's Troop want with me?"

Twisting around, Sibley reached into a saddlebag and withdrew an envelope. Extending it to the gang leader, he told him, "This letter will explain everything, sir."

Colden accepted it. "Climb down and come inside, kid."

Ushered into the cabin and seated at the table, young Sibley looked somewhat intimidated by the motley crew of men collected about him. Colden sat and poured himself another glass of whiskey, then opened the envelope, reading it silently. When he had finished, he was smiling broadly.

Emptying the shot glass in two gulps, he looked around at the group and explained, "We've got us a very temptin' offer here, boys. You all know about those gold and silver mines in Esmeralda County. Well, it seems there's a claims dispute goin' on between the two biggest mines, the Young America and the Winne-

mucca. Mr. Troop of the Young America wants to hire
some . . . 'enforcers.' Says Mr. Uzelac of the Winnemucca
brought in six hired guns to stack the cards in his favor,
and they've already caused Mr. Troop some serious
problems—especially when they murdered his partner
a few days ago."

"Sounds like those Winnemucca boys play rough,
boss," remarked Vince Denning. "You ain't gonna mess
with it, are you? I mean with what we already got goin'
here."

Colden chuckled and replied, "Gettin' rich is our
chief goal, ain't it, Vince?"

"You bet."

"Way it looks, we'll get a whole lot richer a whole lot
faster if we take Mr. Troop up on his offer."

"Aw, come on, Judd," Denning scoffed. "You're tellin' me we can do better than the setup we've got goin'
here in San Andreas?"

Handing him the letter, Colden suggested, "Take a
look. You think you can pocket that kind of money as
fast in San Andreas?"

Denning quickly read Troop's offer, and surprise
showed on his face. "I guess not! When do we leave?"

"What's he offerin' us, boss?" asked Bob Reedy.

"A plenty generous deal, but Troop only wants me
and five men. He says if he hired any more, it would
look like too much of a show of force to the law."

"The law bein' Sheriff Jess Packard," put in Jocko
Bane.

"Yeah," Colden said dryly. "We'll probably end up
havin' to deal with Mr. Packard before things're over
with. Anyway, Troop's offerin' us fifty thousand dollars
up front just for comin', and he'll also cut us in on a
share of the mine's profits. I'll take fourteen thousand,
so that'll leave nine of you to split the rest. That's four
thousand apiece up front. Not too bad, eh?"

Over the exclamations of the others, Reedy asked, "Who'll be goin' with you?"

"Well, since there'd be trouble right off if you, Lloyd, Wes, and Franklin showed up in Packard's town—you know, 'cause of that Indian thing—it'd be best if I take the rest of the boys while you guys hole up here. I'll send your cut by stagecoach, and you can relax awhile. Look at it this way: We'll take over Aurora instead of San Andreas . . . only we'll get even richer because of the gold and silver there. Once I'm in control and have my own man in as sheriff, you and the boys can ride over the mountains and join us."

While the men were agreeing with Colden's plan, Reedy remarked, "I'm not tryin' to tell you what to do, Judd, but you'd best be real careful with Jess Packard. You know his reputation."

"If I might put in a word here," Curt Sibley meekly said, "I'd have to agree with your friend. I live in Aurora, so I've had lots of opportunities to watch Sheriff Packard operate. The man is invincible."

Colden laughed heartily. "There ain't a man on this earth that I fear, kid. That includes Jess Packard."

Denning spoke up, "Coincidentally, it just so happens that I was a boyhood friend of Jess's younger brother, Alex. He and I went to school together in Kansas, so I've seen Jess a few times. I can tell you this: He ain't so much. There's nothin' supernatural about him. He can be killed just like that Marshal Wiley."

Colden laughed, tossing his lank black hair. Looking at Sibley, he told him, "See there, kid? There ain't nothin' for us to worry about." Tilting back his chair, the gang leader slapped his knee. "Well, there are a few loose ends to tie up here—like drawin' our money out of the bank—but I figure we can ride out by late mornin' tomorrow." Turning back to Sibley, he asked,

"You want to head out early, kid, or you want to ride with us?"

"I guess I'll ride with you, sir," the youth replied.

"Fine. Well, boys, let's head into town and eat us a hearty supper, then have us a last good time at the Border Saloon."

Chapter Five

By noon the next day, Judd Colden, his five cohorts, and Curt Sibley were riding high in the Sierras, heading toward the crest of Sonora Pass and the lofty saw-toothed peaks to the east. Glistening with snow that was beginning its spring runoff, the mountain range was dotted with giant glaciers pocketed in the ragged shoulders of the higher mountains, and the sonorous, ever-present wind in the crowns of the towering conifers was like the rush of a distant waterfall.

Pushing his horse up the winding trail behind the outlaws, Curt Sibley thought of the day when Virgil Troop had rescued him from certain death at the hands of the Indians. The youth had been Troop's virtual slave ever since, and often the ruthless man had forced Sibley to do things that violated his conscience. He had frequently entertained the idea of running away, but he owed Troop his life—and besides, Troop would no doubt chase him down. He had no choice but to dance on the mineowner's string.

Having to toady to a man like Judd Colden and listen to his boasting about killing people in cold blood sickened the youth, but feeling there was nothing he could do, he tried to make the best of it. He straggled a few lengths behind the others, taking in the awesome sights around him and deliberately paying no attention to the conversations among the outlaws.

The hours seemed to drag as the sun worked its way across the clear sky, but finally it began to descend, and the shadows ahead of the riders were growing lengthy as the crest of Sonora Pass came into view. They lost sight of it a few times while twisting over the rough switchbacks that zigzagged the final mile before topping the pass, but finally, with the sun almost down, they crested the pass and the McGuire Way Station came into view.

"We'll take rooms for the night there," Colden advised, "and ride to Aurora in the mornin'."

There were two horses tied to the hitch rail by the Station's porch, and a Wells Fargo stagecoach was parked nearby. The team had been unhitched, indicating that the passengers and crew were also staying the night.

The gang stepped inside, their boots scraping and rumbling on the floor. Two men were at the bar, and it seemed likely that the horses tied outside belonged to them. They only glanced casually at the newcomers, but the four well-dressed men sitting and talking at a table in the eating area near the big fireplace regarded the motley bunch with undisguised disdain. At an adjacent table, two aging men who had the look of a stage driver and shotgunner, also looked upon the gang with something less than admiration.

Along with her aunt Mamie, Angie McGuire cooked and waited on tables. She had just taken the order from the stagecoach passengers and crew and was headed for the kitchen when the Colden bunch walked in. Her brilliant auburn hair and curvaceous figure caught Jocko Bane's attention.

Everett McGuire pushed through the curtains of a small office behind the counter and ran his gaze over the faces of the gang. When he saw Curt Sibley among them, a smile brightened his face. "Hello, young fella," he said amiably. "Do you want your horse now, or are you going to stay for the night?"

"I'm staying," replied Sibley, returning the smile. "I'm . . . ah . . . traveling with these gentlemen. They'll be staying, too."

Colden was aware of the looks he and his men were getting from the stagecoach passengers. When McGuire asked if they preferred single or double accommodations, the gang leader disregarded the hostility he felt from the travelers and replied, "Pair these six guys off two to a room, and I'll take a room by myself."

"All right," McGuire responded, clearly wondering why young Sibley was in the company of such rough-looking men. "That'll be two dollars for your friends, and three dollars for the private room."

When each man had paid, Colden said to his cronies, "Okay, boys, let's see what kind of cookin' they've got in this place."

While the gang and Sibley were walking over into the eating area, McGuire crossed the room to the bar, asking the two riders if they wanted anything else to drink. They declined, and downing the last of their whiskey, they turned and headed for the door.

McGuire's wife, Mamie—who was nearing fifty—came from the kitchen carrying a tray with empty cups and a steaming pot of coffee. While she set the cups before the stage crew and the passengers, the gang members took adjoining tables, with the massive Bane sitting with Colden, Sibley, and Denning, while Blanford, Ortiz, and Locke sat together. Casting a hungry glance toward the kitchen door, Bane asked Mamie, "Hey, lady, where's that cute little gal I saw a couple of minutes ago?"

McGuire reached the counter in front of his office and shot a hard glance at the giant, then looked at his wife, who replied, "If you're referring to my niece, mister, she's in the kitchen."

"Well, when I'm served," Bane said, "I want *her* to do it."

At that moment Angie pushed her way through the kitchen door, carrying a tray filled with water glasses. When she moved beside her aunt and began setting the glasses before the stage crew and passengers, Bane pushed his hat to the back of his head and called, "Hey, Red, I want you to be my waitress."

Looking at him coldly, Angie responded, "My aunt and I work together, sir, both in the cooking and the waiting of tables." With that, she returned to the kitchen with Mamie, but soon Angie reappeared, a pad in her hand. Standing between the tables of the motley bunch, purposely out of Jocko Bane's reach, she stated, "I'll take your orders, gentlemen, then bring you coffee."

The last man to order was Bane, and he raised a hand and motioned with a finger for Angie to step closer. "Come over here, honey," he said with a salacious grin that exhibited his crooked, yellow teeth. "I could order easier if I didn't have to yell it."

Angie shook her head firmly, sending her auburn curls into a cascade, and responded flatly, "I can hear you from where I stand. Which will it be? Chicken or beef?"

"I ain't sure," he answered, chuckling. "Why don't you come over here and sit on my lap while I decide?"

Though Bane's repellent looks and dreadful smell were repugnant to the redhead, she decided to do her best to ward off his verbal advances courteously. Glancing over at her uncle and seeing him watching with a look of concern, she gave him a slight, reassuring smile. Angie then gazed back at her huge customer and replied, smiling, "No, thank you. My boyfriend wouldn't like it."

"Oh, so you've got a boyfriend!" He guffawed, then snorted, "Where is he? I'll chew him up and spit him out!"

"You aren't man enough," Angie retorted tartly.

The giant bristled at the redhead's response. "I ain't man enough, eh?"

"How tall are you?" she asked.

"Six-four—without my boots."

"And how much do you weigh?"

"Three hundred."

She laughed, taunting him, "You're a dwarf! My boyfriend is seven feet tall and weighs four hundred pounds . . . and if he found out I sat on your lap, he'd pound you into mincemeat!"

"Aw, go on!" Bane blustered. "When a man that big walks through the door, I'll sit here with my mouth shut! There ain't no such fella."

Angie mocked, "Shucks, you were smart enough to figure that out! Well, let me put it like this: When a man that size walks through the door, I'll sit on your lap—and not until!"

Judd Colden broke into a hearty laugh that was so contagious, soon the rest of his men were laughing. Angie again glanced at her uncle, and found him smiling and relaxed behind the counter, and the men from the stagecoach who sat nearby began to chuckle as well. The tension in the room had eased.

"That's pretty good, little lady!" Mel Blanford laughed. "I guess you put Jocko in his place!"

Smiling, Angie looked at Bane and told him, "I'll put you down for chicken. You look hungry for chicken."

She started for the kitchen, brushing past the huge man, but Bane reached out and seized her arm. Suddenly the room was again filled with tension.

Angie tried to squirm loose, but the big man gripped her tight and pulled her to his side. His stench was nauseating. "Let go of me," she demanded through clenched teeth.

"Not till I feel like it," Bane countered. "I think I'm about to get me a great big kiss."

McGuire started around the counter toward his niece, but suddenly one of the stagecoach passengers left his table, clearly intent on rescuing Angie. In his midthirties and muscular, the traveler was a good deal shorter and at least a hundred pounds lighter than Bane.

"Pardon me," the man said as he drew up. "Jocko is your name, is that right?"

Bane gave the man a black stare. "Yeah. So what?" replied the giant, looking up at him while maintaining his grip on Angie's arm.

"I like to address a man by his name," came the traveler's reply. "My name is Jim Tasker."

"Well, now, I'm all excited about that," came the mocking growl.

"I've come over here to ask you politely to stop bothering the young lady, Jocko," Tasker said levelly with no trace of fear in his voice.

"Besides, Jocko," Colden said in an obvious attempt to defuse the situation, "I'm hungry, and we ain't gonna get our food till you let her do her work. Let her go."

Bane regarded his leader for a long moment, then reluctantly freed Angie.

Rubbing her arm, Angie stepped away from the giant and called to the passenger, who was already returning to his table, "Thank you, Mr. Tasker. I appreciate your help."

Pausing by his chair, Tasker smiled and responded, "You're most welcome, Miss McGuire."

The way-station owner walked over to his niece and put a protective arm around her as he addressed Tasker. "I'm beholden to you, too, sir."

Shooting a sharp glance at Bane, Tasker remarked,

"It isn't in my makeup to stand idly by at such a scene. I can't stand dirty drifters who push themselves on nice young women."

The giant's head whipped around as he heard the remark, and he rose to his feet. His temper flaring, he kicked back his chair and stomped toward Tasker, snarling, "Dirty drifter, eh?"

The other onlookers leapt from their chairs and headed for the walls to avoid the imminent fight. Mamie stood frozen in the kitchen doorway, and her husband hurried toward her, taking Angie with him to safety.

Surprising the giant, Tasker clipped Bane on the chin, popping his huge head back. But while it rocked him, it did no particular damage, and Bane countered by leaping at his opponent, mauling and clawing Tasker as he took the man to the floor with his overwhelming weight.

The combatants wrestled in the middle of the room, with the passenger every once in a while getting in a good lick but for the most part Bane having the clear advantage. Tasker finally wriggled free and got to his feet; however, the giant immediately followed suit, and the battle resumed, with Bane clearly enjoying the upper hand.

Angie stiffened and grasped her uncle's arm as Bane repeatedly pummeled her rescuer. When the huge man kicked Tasker in the stomach, she winced in sympathy, unable to imagine the terrible pain. Looking at the other passengers, she realized as they stood flat against the wall that none of them had the courage—or perhaps recklessness—to get into the fight, and the stage driver and his partner were simply too old.

The beautiful redhead hesitated asking her uncle to help because Everett McGuire was aging and never had been a strong man, physically. Jocko Bane might well cripple him.

Angie was repulsed by how the giant's rowdy friends were shouting encouragement, fueling Bane's determination to turn Jim Tasker into pulp. Still, she was surprised at how well the muscular passenger was holding his own—and even giving a lot back.

Her breath suddenly caught in her throat. Tasker had almost done Bane in with his last punch. Unaware that she was behaving much like the giant's cronies, she doubled both fists and shook them, shouting, "One more, Mr. Tasker! One more is all it'll take! Give him another one just like the last one!"

But Jim Tasker did not have another punch left, and his hands suddenly fell limply to his sides.

Suddenly McGuire charged in and stood in front of Bane. "That's enough!" he commanded, throwing up his hands as if warding off evil. "Take your friends and get out of here!"

Enraged, the giant hit McGuire and sent him rolling. McGuire lay against the rough rock base of the fireplace, barely moving. Angie and Mamie screamed, but while her aunt stood frozen with fear, the young woman saw red and flew into action. Dashing into the kitchen, she grabbed a heavy, cast-iron skillet from a hook on the wall and, hefting it like a club, hurried back into the main room.

Racing across to the giant so unexpectedly that none of Bane's friends had time to call out a warning, Angie whacked him over the head with the skillet and knocked him out cold.

Mamie ran to her husband and knelt beside him as he slowly came to. Still holding the skillet in her right hand, Angie helped her uncle sit up with her left.

McGuire rose shakily to his feet and glared at Judd Colden. Rubbing his head, he demanded, "Take your repulsive friend out of here and leave. You and your bunch are not welcome. I'll give you your money back."

Clearly weary from the long ride and needing rest, the gang leader responded, "Look, Mr. McGuire, my men won't cause you no more trouble. I'm real sorry for what happened"—he smiled placatingly—"but I'm afraid my pal Jocko gets out of hand now and then. I'd like to ask you to reconsider and let us stay."

A loud groan behind them indicated that the man in question was stirring.

Looking at his niece, McGuire remarked, "This all started over you, honey. How do you feel about it?"

Angie ran her gaze over the faces of the odious bunch, looked at Jim Tasker, then finally replied, "If you want to let them stay, Uncle Everett, it's all right with me. But I think that awful brute should be made to apologize to Mr. Tasker."

From where he sat across the room, nursing his bruised and battered body, Tasker shook his head. "Don't concern yourself with me, Miss McGuire. You're the one he ought to apologize to."

"He's right about that, Ev," Mamie agreed. "If that dreadful man is going to stay under our roof, he should beg Angie's forgiveness for the way he talked to her and for putting his dirty hands on her."

McGuire looked at Colden and waited for his comment. The gang leader rubbed the back of his neck and agreed, "Yeah, he was out of line—and like I said, we don't want no more trouble here."

Bane was now sitting up and gingerly examining the huge knot on the back of his head. His split lip was still trickling blood. Looking at Colden, he asked, "What happened?"

"The little redhead whacked you with a skillet when you went after her uncle," Colden replied. "And now you're gonna apologize to her for the way you treated her."

Gritting his teeth angrily, Bane said flatly, "I ain't apologizin' to her for nothin'."

Colden leaned over and helped his huge friend to his feet, advising, "If you don't, we ain't gonna be able to stay here tonight—and that won't make me none too happy."

The slight tone of menace in Colden's voice made it quite clear that Jocko Bane would regret it if he did not do as his boss said. The apology was made, and the men all sat down at the tables, while the women returned to the kitchen to prepare more food. Bane and Tasker exchanged hard looks but no words.

As soon as the food was brought, the minimal talk among the men subsided, and they ate ravenously. While the meal was in progress, the station owner went outside to tend the horses, and as soon as McGuire was gone, the giant gazed toward the kitchen, where Angie was working with her aunt.

Presently, the women emerged from the kitchen, with Angie carrying a tray of biscuits and Mamie holding a steaming coffeepot. While Mamie was pouring coffee for the stage passengers, Angie served up biscuits to Colden, Bane, Sibley, and Denning.

Casting a quick glance toward the door, the giant suddenly grabbed the redhead by the waist and pulled her onto his lap. When she squealed in protest, Mamie wheeled around, and the travelers looked over.

Squirming against Bane's powerful grip, Angie shrieked, "Let me go!"

"Aw, now, honey," Bane responded. "You see this cut on my lip? I bet it'd heal quicker if you were to press those luscious lips against it."

Twisting forcefully, Angie broke the huge man's hold and slipped out of his grasp. He reached for her, and she slapped his face violently with her free hand, then tossed the contents of her tray in his face. Bane merely laughed and lunged out of the chair, gripping her shoulders, and the tray clattered to the floor.

"You beast!" she railed, slapping him again.

"You're sure some spitfire!" Bane said with a laugh, pulling her toward him.

Angie wrenched loose, but his powerful fingers ripped her dress, exposing a milky shoulder. Screaming in fear and anger, the redhead backed away from him, covering her bare skin with her hand.

Just as he reached for her again, Mamie McGuire picked up a cup she had just filled with steaming coffee and tossed it directly in Bane's face. He screeched and wiped his eyes, then glared murderously at Mamie.

The woman began backtracking, fear evident in her eyes, as Bane swore and started for her. Suddenly Curt Sibley stepped in front of her to protect her and stared at the giant.

Towering over the youth, Bane snarled, "Get outta the way, kid!"

"I don't want to fight you, Jocko," Sibley responded, his voice breaking, "but I'm asking you not to hurt her."

From across the room, Colden warned, "Better not irritate him, kid, 'cause nothin' I could say to him at this point will make any difference. If he ain't allowed to work out some of his frustration, he'll become like a wild animal—so if you make him mad, you'll surely regret it." Eyeing the travelers, the gang leader asserted, "That goes for you, too."

Bane regarded Sibley with mocking contempt and promised, "If I have to move you, I'll break both your arms."

His face turning pale, Sibley fearfully stepped aside, and the other men were equally intimidated. Laughing, Bane slapped Mamie hard with an open hand, knocking her to the floor. Then, before Angie could escape, the giant grabbed her and planted a lingering kiss on her mouth. The redhead bit down hard on his lip, drawing more blood, and the giant screamed with rage and started to choke her.

Just then Angie's uncle entered. Seeing his wife lying stunned on the floor and his niece in danger, McGuire dashed across the room and jumped on the giant's back, digging his fingers into Bane's eyes.

Bane roared and threw Angie across the room, where she slammed into a wall and slumped to the floor. The huge man then wrestled McGuire to the floor and began pummeling the much smaller man.

When the stage driver and his partner started going for their revolvers, Judd Colden whipped out his gun and cocked it, snapping, "Don't do it! You'll die if you do!" The rest of the gang pulled out their guns as well, and as they covered the group of travelers, Colden sent Vince Denning to confiscate the crew's weapons and any that the passengers had. The travelers watched helplessly as Jocko Bane began slamming Ev McGuire's head against the stone base of the fireplace.

Finally gaining her feet, Mamie looked over and saw what the giant was doing to her husband, and she shrieked in horror. Turning toward Colden, she implored, "Stop him! Stop him! He'll kill Ev!"

But the gang leader merely shrugged. "Nothin' I can do, lady. Jocko's too far gone now. I'd get *my* head slammed if I tried to interfere"—he grinned—"and I sure don't want that."

Turning to her niece, Mamie helped the stunned redhead to her feet, and both women realized that if the brutality was going to be stopped, *they* were going to have to stop it. They dashed through the kitchen door and into the pantry, where McGuire kept a pair of always-loaded shotguns. Grabbing them, they ran back into the main room and trained the weapons on the gang.

"Drop those guns and raise your hands, or I'll shoot!" Angie commanded, her dark blue eyes flashing. The outlaws spun around and stared at her, and it was evident from the expression on her face that she meant business. They let their guns slip to the floor, then raised their hands.

At the same time, Mamie dashed to Jocko Bane and jammed the muzzle of the twelve-gauge against the back of his neck. "Stop it, or I'll blow your rotten head off!" she bellowed.

Bane immediately complied and backed away, joining his cohorts.

The stage passengers gathered the outlaws' guns and, training the weapons on the gang, forced them to leave the station and warned them not to return. Furious, the gang saddled their horses and rode off.

Mamie and Angie were frantic. The unconscious McGuire was bleeding from numerous gashes, and they needed to get him to the doctor in Bridgeport, some eighteen miles away at the foot of the Sierras.

"I sure wish we could help you ladies out," the stage driver told them, "but we're due in Placerville to the west tomorrow, and if we don't show up, why, the whole schedule from here to the California coast gets thrown off."

Nodding, Mamie assured him, "I understand. We'll take Everett to Bridgeport in our wagon."

"I'd be willing to interrupt my trip and ride with you for protection, in case that gang shows up again," Jim Tasker offered.

"Thank you kindly, Mr. Tasker," Mamie responded, "but I'm not worried about that. We'll take our shotguns with us, and since they're unarmed, those fellas wouldn't dare approach us. However, you can help us by taking a horse and riding to our closest neighbor, about a mile south of here, and ask him to come and take care of the station while we're gone. Meanwhile, Angie and I'll bandage my husband as best we can to stop the bleeding."

The traveler readily complied.

When Tasker and the neighbor returned, Mamie and Angie left the station in the neighbor's hands, and with McGuire laid in the back of their wagon, they headed east down Sonora Pass. Only a sliver of a moon was visible in the star-studded sky, making the going treacherous and slow. Angie drove the wagon while Mamie rode in the bed, her husband's head cradled in her lap while she prayed that he would not die.

Chapter Six

The gang rode northwest through the High Sierras, picking their way carefully along a path through the pines and heading toward a cabin that Judd Colden knew about. On his horse behind the gang leader's, Jocko Bane muttered, "Judd, we gotta find some weapons somewhere and go back to that way station. I'm for killin' everybody there."

"There ain't no place around here to get weapons, Jocko," Colden rejoined. "We'll have to get 'em down in Bridgeport, and by the time we get there, we'll be practically to Aurora. We need to report in to Virgil Troop tomorrow. We'll come back to the way station and take care of the McGuires later."

As Colden led his men down a narrow path that would bottom out at a small stream, Vince Denning asked, "How come you know about this cabin back in here, Judd?"

"I've been in this country a lot," Colden replied, "and I happened upon the place one time when I was takin' a shortcut toward Sonora Pass from the north. Holed up there durin' a snowstorm for a couple of days. I think fur trappers built it."

Suddenly the aroma of wood smoke wafted through the pines, and the gang leader pulled rein and stared through the tall trees. After a moment, he swore.

Denning asked, "What's the matter?"

Colden growled, "The smoke you smell is coming from the cabin I've been talkin' about. Somebody's in it!"

"We can throw 'em out," Gene Ortiz suggested.

"Hey, maybe they got weapons!" Bane exclaimed hopefully. "We can take 'em away from 'em and go back to the way station!"

"Let's take it one step at a time," Colden snapped, nudging his horse down the steep path. "First thing is to see who's in the cabin."

The gang rode to a spot within thirty yards of the cabin and dismounted. Colden then left his men and Curt Sibley in the brush while he crept up to the cabin that was nestled in a stand of tall trees. The windows glowed yellow with lantern light, and smoke rose from the chimney in thin tendrils. After cautiously looking in the windows, Colden returned and told his men that three trappers were in the cabin. All of them wore revolvers, and there were rifles leaning against one wall.

Leaving young Sibley with the horses, Colden ushered his men to a stand of young pines near the front door of the cabin. Their plan was to lure the trappers outside and then club them with tree limbs. Choosing some suitable limbs from where they lay scattered on the ground, Bane, Denning, Blanford, Ortiz, and Locke flattened themselves against the front of the cabin on either side of the door.

When his men were in place, Colden scurried to a spot twenty feet from the door and lay down on the ground. Then, in a mournful wail, he cried, "Help! Help me!"

A scooting of chairs on the wooden floor of the cabin could be heard, followed by the sound of footsteps. The door came open, and Colden repeated his cry for help.

The trapper who had opened the door turned and told his partners that a man was outside on the ground, and the others hurried to join him.

When all the trappers had stepped outside and started toward Colden, the outlaws let loose with their clubs from behind them, bashing the trappers' heads until they were dead. Ortiz was sent to get Sibley and the horses while the rest of the gang dragged the bodies to a nearby cliff and tossed them over the edge.

When Colden and the others returned to the cabin, Ortiz and Sibley were waiting. The youth was visibly upset, and he accosted Colden, demanding, "Why did you have to kill them? They might have welcomed us into the cabin with no trouble at all. Why do you have to be so heartless and brutal?"

Judd Colden slapped the youth across the face and bellowed, "Don't you question me, kid! This bunch does things my way, and nobody speaks out against it! All you are is a messenger boy, so keep your mouth shut!"

Sibley put a hand to his stinging cheek and mumbled, "I'm sorry. I just thought—"

"Well, don't think! I'm the one who does the thinkin' around here—and don't forget it!"

The youth nodded silently and followed the outlaws into the cabin. As they settled in, Jocko Bane remarked, "Look, Judd, we've got guns now. Let's stop at the way station in the mornin' and kill them McGuires before we head down the pass."

"You don't listen too good, Jocko," the gang leader retorted. "Like I said, we'll take care of the McGuires at some later time; we've got to get to the Young America mine as quick as we can. Got that?"

Bane nodded. "All right, boss," he said glumly. "We'll get 'em later."

"Good. Now let's all get ourselves a few hours' sleep. We'll head out at dawn."

The sun's first rays were rising over the rugged hills to the east as Angie McGuire drove the wagon onto the still-deserted main street of Bridgeport. Hauling the wagon to a stop in front of the doctor's office, Angie jumped to the ground and glanced into the bed. Everett McGuire, his head still in his wife's lap, was conscious, but he was in a great deal of pain.

Hurrying up the steps, Angie turned the doorknob but found it locked. Frantic, she pounded on the door. Presently the door opened, revealing a thin, middle-aged woman who identified herself as the doctor's wife. After Angie described her uncle's condition, the woman apologetically explained that her husband was out of town for several days and advised that the patient be taken to Aurora, the next closest town with a doctor. Having no other choice, the desperate young woman drove as quickly as she could for the Nevada line and Aurora.

It was midmorning when their wagon rolled into Aurora and swung onto Pine Street. Since none of the McGuires had ever been to the boomtown, Angie pulled rein and stopped the first person she saw to ask directions to Dr. Jacob Wren's office.

"Excuse me, sir!" she called to a tall man walking across the street, carrying a tray. The man turned, and she saw that he wore a badge. "Oh! You're the sheriff," Angie remarked.

"That's right. Sheriff Jess Packard."

"I wonder if you can tell me where the clinic is. My uncle's in real bad shape."

Packard stepped over to the wagon, and his eyes widened at the sight of the couple in the wagon bed. A blood-soaked cloth in the older woman's hand was pressed to her husband's head, and it was obvious that the man was in dire need of medical assistance. A light of recognition appeared in the lawman's eyes, and he exclaimed, "Mrs. McGuire! What happened to your husband? And why did you come all the way to Aurora for help?"

"Bridgeport's doctor is out of town, Sheriff," Mamie McGuire replied anxiously. "We had no choice but to come all the way here."

"I'll take you to Dr. Wren's office myself," the lawman responded quickly. Looking around, he hailed a man on the boardwalk, who hurried over to him. Handing him the tray, Packard explained, "This is Hugo Stern's breakfast. Would you take it to him for me? The office door is unlocked. Just slide the tray under Stern's cell door."

"Will do," the man promised and went on his way.

Packard jumped onto the seat beside Angie and directed, "Straight up the street, miss. I'll tell you when to stop."

When they reached the doctor's office, Packard suggested, "You ladies go on ahead and tell Dr. Wren what's going on. I'll carry Mr. McGuire in."

While the women hurried inside, the lawman gathered McGuire into his arms and carried him into the clinic. The physician directed Packard to lay the station owner on the examining table, and his wife—who was also his nurse and who, like her husband, was in her early fifties—started laying out his instruments. Dr. Wren took a quick look at his patient, then told Angie and Mamie, "Make yourselves comfortable in the waiting room. This is going to take a while."

The redhead and the sheriff turned to leave, but Mamie gave the doctor a pleading look and asked, "If I were to sit over here, could I stay?"

Wren gave his permission, and the harried woman sat in a chair in the corner. Packard opened the door for Angie, then followed her out, closing the door behind him. Standing over her as she dropped onto a chair, he asked, "Now, do you want to tell me what happened to your uncle?"

"All right," she replied, smiling weakly. "I'm Angie McGuire—my father was Uncle Everett's brother—and I've been staying with my aunt and uncle for a couple of months. At any rate—" She suddenly began to cry, and Packard put a comforting arm around her shoulder. After a few moments, she sniffed and continued, "It was awful, Sheriff. Have you ever heard of a man named Judd Colden? I'm sure he has to be an outlaw."

The lawman's expression hardened. "Colden," he muttered, saying the name as though it left a bad taste in his mouth. "Yeah, he's an outlaw, all right. He was responsible for your uncle's injuries?"

Angie slowly gave Packard the details of the incident at the way station, showing her own distaste for huge Jocko Bane. When she had told him the entire story, the sheriff shook his head and said, "I'll say this, miss. You ladies have shown what genuine courage is all about."

Angie shrugged. "We just did what we had to do, Sheriff."

"Yeah, but taking on a tough bunch of men like the Colden gang . . . Whew! I'm impressed!"

Blushing slightly, the redhead changed the subject—and turned the tables. "I read about you in one of the Denver newspapers, Sheriff. It seems you're quite famous for the way you handle outlaws and troublemakers."

It was Packard's turn to shrug. "I just . . . ah . . . do what I have to do," he said, echoing Angie's words.

Looking into the lawman's dark brown eyes, Angie

asked, "Did a fellow named Hank Wesson show up here?"

"Yes, he did. Yesterday. How did you know he was coming?"

"He was at the way station the day before, boasting that he was going to ride to Aurora and shoot you. Did . . . did you have to kill him?"

"I'm afraid so."

"I'm not surprised. Everyone at the station told him he'd be a fool to try drawing against you. One of them—a young man named Sibley, who was with the Colden gang last night—said he was from Aurora and that you were hired by this tough town for a reason. Wesson only laughed it off." She was quiet for a moment, then added, "It was strange about that young man. He actually stood up to that horrible giant, Jocko Bane, and tried to intercede in our behalf."

The lawman's face mottled with anger. That Curt Sibley was riding with the gang meant only one thing: Virgil Troop had sent Sibley to California to hire the notorious outlaw and his henchmen as strong arms for his mine.

Cocking her head and peering at Packard, Angie remarked, "From the look on your face, apparently something I just said has upset you."

The sheriff sighed and explained about the trouble between the Young America and Winnemucca mines, adding, "Colden isn't simply a bodyguard, he's a cold and heartless killer. So are the men who run with him. The man is so crafty, he's eluded the law all over the West, for none of the killings he's committed have been pinned on him. His arrival is going to mean far more trouble in Aurora."

"I can certainly testify to that," Angie muttered, rising to her feet. "Excuse me for a moment. I want to check on Uncle Everett."

Standing himself, Packard watched the lovely red-head enter the surgery room. When the door closed behind her, he sat back down, realizing that he found himself a bit taken with Angie McGuire's spunk, warmth, and beauty.

When Angie returned a few moments later, she said, "The doctor hasn't finished yet." As she sat down, she smiled at the lawman and remarked, "You must have things to do, Sheriff. Please don't let me detain you."

"I have three deputies on duty," he said softly, "and they're keeping their eyes on the town. One of them saw me carrying your uncle in here, so if they need me, they know where to find me."

Angie smiled. "It's nice of you to keep me company."

"When someone you love is in surgery, it helps to have company," Packard replied. Studying her, he asked, "What did you do in Denver?"

"I was a bookkeeper in a bank."

"Seems like a beautiful young woman like yourself would be married by now."

Angie's face showed pain, and tears filled her eyes.

Packard said hastily, "Oh, I'm sorry. I can see I just struck a nerve. Please forgive me. Me and my big mouth."

Shaking her head, she wiped away the tears, saying, "No, please. Don't blame yourself. Your comment was only natural. Most women my age are married by now, and I would have been, too, if—"

"Some man broke your heart, didn't he?"

"You might say that," she answered, sniffing. "I was engaged to a man I thought loved me. Four days before the wedding he suddenly announced that it was over between us, and he was going to marry one of Denver's socialites. In other words, he jilted me to marry a rich woman."

"He's the loser," Packard commented quietly. "Is that why you left Denver to live with your aunt and uncle?"

"Yes. Both my parents are dead, so I came to live with Aunt Mamie and Uncle Everett to try to put my life back together."

"I'm sorry for the heartache you've had. That was a low-down thing for that fella to do—although you're obviously better off without a skunk like that. I sure hope things'll turn out well for you in the future."

"Thank you," she said, giving him a sad smile. "And you, Sheriff. Do you have a family?"

"Not yet," he replied softly. "I'm working on it, though. I'm getting married next month."

"Oh, you are? And who's the lucky woman?"

He reddened. "Well, I don't know if she's lucky or not, but her name's Monica Wood. Her father owns one of the newspapers here in town, the *Aurora Times*."

Despite her recent betrayal, Angie found the handsome lawman very fascinating and wished he were not engaged. Masking those feelings, she smiled and told him, "I hope you'll be very happy."

Just then the door to the surgery room opened and Jacob Wren entered the waiting room with Mamie right behind him. Wren informed Angie and the sheriff that he was able to stop the bleeding, and that apart from a few scars, Everett McGuire would be as good as new in time. Relieved, the redhead hugged her aunt.

The physician put a hand on Mamie's shoulder, adding, "Mrs. McGuire, I'd like to examine my patient in a week to make sure he's healing properly. Can you bring him back?"

"We can manage that, Doctor," Mamie assured him.

The physician's fee was paid, and with Jess Packard's help, the station owner was once again placed in the wagon bed. Mamie climbed in beside her husband, and preparing to leave, Angie stood next to the wagon, thanking Packard for all his help and for his company.

"It was my pleasure, Miss McGuire," the rugged lawman responded with a smile.

Helping the redhead onto the driver's seat, Packard was about to say good-bye when a rumble of hoofbeats sounded from the north end of the street. He turned around and saw seven riders heading their way, Curt Sibley among them, and knew he was looking at the nefarious Colden gang.

He glanced at the McGuires and saw them tense. Stepping to the center of the street, Packard raised a hand, signaling for the riders to stop, and they reluctantly pulled rein. The lawman gave Sibley a look of disgust for being in such company, then asked, "Which one of you is Colden?"

Packard noted that the gang members were glaring maliciously at the McGuires, and he snapped louder, "I asked which one of you is Colden!"

The gang leader churlishly answered, "I'm Judd Colden."

Packard's eyes bored into the man as he railed, "I've been told what you did to these people at the way station. Mr. McGuire almost bled to death!"

Gesturing at the massive man beside him, Colden declared, "Jocko did it on his own, Sheriff. There was nothin' I could do to stop him."

The lawman stared at Bane, then mocked, "Do you always pick on men half your size and twice your age? Seems to me you're the worst kind of coward. I'll bet there's a yellow stripe down your back a foot wide."

The giant merely laughed. "You can say whatever you want, lawman, and it don't matter none, 'cause you know that what I did to them people was in California and you ain't got no jurisdiction there. Ain't a blessed thing you can do about it."

Packard had to work hard to fight down the impulse to pull the man off his horse and smash his face. Red with anger, he rasped, "If you ever bother these people again, I'll forget all about jurisdiction. That's a promise. And that goes for all of you, understand?"

The outlaws looked at each other, then nodded at Packard. "We understand, Sheriff," replied Colden, nudging his horse to move on. The others immediately followed suit.

But Packard grabbed the reins of Colden's horse and snapped, "I'm not done talking to you!" Turning to the wagon, he suggested, "You go ahead and pull out, Miss McGuire. I'll see you folks when you return."

Smiling and waving good-bye, Angie then clucked to the team and wheeled the wagon around on the broad street, skirting the outlaws and heading west. As she drove away, she thought that she had never seen such a handsome and charming man—nor had anyone ever had such an effect on her. Something strange was definitely happening in her heart. Mentioning it to her aunt, she remarked, "But I'm a fool for letting myself feel something for him. After all, he's practically married."

Mamie chuckled and retorted, "There's a big difference between married and *practically* married, honey. And from the look in that man's eyes when he was talking with you, I'd say there's an even bigger difference!"

Turning his attention from the McGuire wagon to the men on horseback, Sheriff Packard eyed Colden coldly and said, "Since Curt is with you, I assume you're the ones Virgil Troop has hired as his hatchet men."

"Now, wait a minute, Sheriff," Colden objected. "We ain't hatchet men. Troop's simply hired us to help keep peace between the Young America and Winnemucca mines."

"Call it what you will, mister," Packard retorted, "but I'll give it to you straight: Cross the line of the law in this county, and you'll be one sorry son. I'm here to uphold the law, and I'll do it no matter who gets bumped, bruised, or killed."

"We'll just do our job for Mr. Troop, Sheriff," Colden replied.

"Fine," Packard responded. "Keep my warning in mind while you're doing it, and we'll all be happy."

The outlaws were about to move on when Vince Denning suddenly exclaimed, "Alex! Alex Packard! I haven't seen you for a long time, old pal!"

The lawman looked around to find his brother standing with his dark-haired wife, Lola, and their two children. He realized from the expression on Alex's face that the younger Packard had been there long enough to hear most of the conversation and knew who the mounted men were. A bit flushed, Alex smiled at Denning and said, "Nice to see you, Vince."

"I'm gonna be workin' at the Young America mine," Denning told him. "We'll get together and talk over old times."

"Sure, Vince," Alex answered, his voice somewhat nervous. "We'll do that."

Colden looked at Denning and grinned. "Well, if you're done greetin' your old friend, what say we go into one of these saloons and wet our whistles before we report to the mine."

A chorus of agreement met the suggestion, and the gang headed farther up the street. Packard watched them until they dismounted in front of a saloon a half block away, then walked over to his brother. Greeting Lola and the children, he then asked Alex, "Who's the gang member who knows you?"

"I didn't know he'd turned outlaw, Jess," Alex responded. "His name's Vince Denning. We were close friends in school, but it was just before you left home. You probably saw him a few times, but I guess you wouldn't remember him."

"He's running with a rough bunch, Alex," the lawman pointed out. "And you know what they say about birds of a feather. Be careful. I mean it."

Chapter Seven

Wanting to have a talk with Virgil Troop while the Colden gang was in the saloon, Sheriff Jess Packard hopped on his horse and galloped to the Young America mine. Troop was just coming out of the mine and heading for the office building as Packard rode up. Swinging from the saddle, the sheriff declared, "I want to talk to you, Virgil."

Halting, the mineowner gave the lawman a sour look. "What is it now?" Troop asked with irritation.

"I just ran into Judd Colden and his bunch in town," Packard answered. "Colden tells me you've hired them as peacemakers."

"So what?" Troop snapped back indignantly.

"Colden and his men are killers, Virgil. I mean cold-blooded murderers. Bringing them here isn't going to bring peace; it'll create a war!"

Troop bristled. "Uzelac hired men to kill my partner, so I'm gonna fight fire with fire!"

"You have no proof that Uzelac's men murdered Web," countered Packard.

"Well, who else would've done it? Tell me that, Packard!"

"I don't know, but it seems to me that if Uzelac had hired those men to kill Web, they'd have come after you, too. If one owner of the Young America was in

Uzelac's way, so is the other one. How come they haven't killed you?"

"I figure they're planning to do just that—which is why I hired Judd Colden and his boys to protect me! You gonna fault me for trying to save my own life?"

"No, I won't fault you for that," responded the sheriff, turning toward his horse. Mounting, he stared unwaveringly at the mineowner, warning, "You've brought in a real pack of wolves, Virgil. If Colden and his men get out of line, I'm holding you directly responsible." Nodding curtly, the sheriff pivoted his horse and trotted off.

Watching Packard leave, Troop swore under his breath. He then wheeled around and headed for his office, slamming the door angrily behind him.

He had been sitting at his desk for a half hour, going over the books, when he heard the rumble of hoofbeats. Looking up from his desk and out the dirt-streaked window, he saw seven riders coming toward the office. He jumped up from his chair and hurried to the door, pulling it open to gaze at the horsemen. Seeing Curt Sibley among them, he knew he was looking at Judd Colden and his men.

Troop expansively welcomed the group, and after introductions were made, everyone filed into the office. Sibley stood in the doorway, leaning on the frame and looking on, while the gang members sat in chairs encircling Troop's desk as the mineowner went to a large safe in the corner behind his desk.

Opening the safe, Troop pulled out a cloth sack and dropped it on the desk. The dull clinking sound indicated the sack's contents. Easing into his chair, Troop looked at Colden and said, "There's your front money as promised—fifty thousand in gold coins."

Colden's eyes lit up, and his men all wore broad smiles. "This relationship is startin' out real good, Virgil," the gang leader declared. "Now, tell me about the percentage of the take."

Reaching in a desk drawer, Troop pulled out a sheet of paper with handwritten columns of figures and handed it to Colden. "This is last year's financial report on the Young America mine. That figure at the bottom right is the gold and silver added together. I have no reason to believe we'll do any less this year. How does five percent of that total sound to you?"

Grinning from ear to ear, Colden replied, "Sounds good!"

"Okay. I'll pay you your percentage once a month."

"What'll that amount to, Judd?" asked Vince Denning.

"Plenty," Colden assured him, chuckling. "I'll go over it with you fellas later. Right now we need to find out about our duties."

Troop explained that during each workday, the men were to mill about outside the mine, keeping their eyes open for trouble. Two of the gang were to stay close to Troop at all times, wherever he went, except at night. The mineowner slept in the bunkhouse with his miners and felt safe there.

"Where'll we stay?" Colden asked.

"I've bought a large house for just that purpose on the outskirts of town. Matter of fact, you can see it from here. I'll point it out when we go outside."

Nodding, Colden asked, "So that's it? Be bodyguards to you and the mine?"

"Essentially. But I'll also need four of your men to escort our gold and silver shipments to Carson City two or three times a month. That'll leave me with two of you here to protect me."

"Fine," Colden agreed. "Vince and I will be the ones to stay with you when the shipments go. When's the next one?"

"Coming right up," Troop replied. "It'll be ready in a couple of days."

Taking the outlaws outside, the mineowner pointed out their new home from the porch of his office. "I'll give you an hour to get settled in," he said. "Then you can get right to work. I'll need two of you to accompany me into town this afternoon. One of my miners is standing trial for murder."

"Is he guilty?" Colden asked, holding the sack of gold coins in his hand.

"Yeah."

"They gonna hang him?"

"I'm afraid so. I tried to get Sheriff Packard to put some pressure on the judge to give Hugo life in prison instead of the noose, but he refused."

"Hardheaded, ain't he?"

"Very."

"Well, I tell you what, Virgil," Colden declared, laying a hand on Troop's shoulder, "we just may have to deal with that lawman."

Troop looked at him levelly and cautioned, "You'd best think about that for a long time before making any moves."

Grinning confidently, Colden responded, "Yeah. I'll do that." He turned to his men and said, "Come on, fellas. Let's go get settled in."

Troop stood beside Curt Sibley while the outlaws mounted and rode down the hill to inspect their new house. When they were out of earshot, the mineowner turned to the youth and told him, "You did a good job, Curt. Things'll be smoother around here now."

"I don't know about that, Mr. Troop," Sibley replied, his voice tremulous.

Peering at him, Troop realized the youth was visibly shaken. "Why do you say that?"

"I'm real concerned abut those men, sir. I saw them

in action on the trip. They are heartless, cold-blooded, and vicious." He described the incident at the way station, then told Troop about the murders of the fur trappers.

Troop snorted. "They're exactly what I need: a real tough outfit. Wait'll Art Uzelac hears that the Colden bunch is working for me. He'll think twice about giving me any more trouble."

At two o'clock that afternoon, Hugo Stern's trial was held. He was quickly convicted of murder, and the judge sentenced him to hang the next day at sunrise.

Virgil Troop was seated between Judd Colden and Vince Denning during the short trial. When the court was dismissed and Sheriff Jess Packard was taking the shackled Stern back to the jail, Troop and his bodyguards caught up with the prisoner. The mineowner told him, "I'm sorry, Hugo. I was hoping the sheriff would ask the judge to give you life in prison, but . . ."

Packard glared at Troop, then growled, "This man murdered one of my deputies. I have no sympathy for murderers"—he shifted his icy gaze to Colden—"no matter who they are."

Colden said nothing, but when the sheriff had led Stern away, he muttered, "I'm tellin' you, Virgil, that man needs to be dealt with."

That evening, Jess Packard and Monica Wood were having dinner at the Sierra Hotel restaurant. Monica had been unusually quiet all through the meal, and she only picked at her food. When Packard was almost finished eating, he looked at her nearly full plate, raised his glance to her face, and asked, "Is something bothering you, honey?"

Laying her fork down, she replied, "As a matter of fact, there is." Monica took a deep breath, then explained, "You didn't notice me, but I happened to be on the street this morning when you helped that red-head into her wagon." Her voice was as cold as ice. "Somebody told me she's Everett McGuire's niece."

"Yes, that's right."

"What's her name?"

"Angie McGuire. Her father was Everett's brother."

"She's quite beautiful, isn't she?" the blonde commented stiffly.

"Yes, I guess she is," he responded honestly.

Jealousy was evident in Monica's eyes and acid was in her tone as she remarked, "I saw how she looked at you just before she drove away."

"What do you mean?"

"Hungrily . . . and dreamy-eyed."

The lawman grinned and snorted. "Aw, come on, honey. That's all in your imagination. She was just being cordial. Why, she barely knows me. We spent a few minutes talking while her uncle was in surgery, that's all."

An angry frown flitted across Monica's face. "My imagination, huh? She was just being cordial, was she? Hah! You men are so blind! Don't tell me it was my imagination. I'm a woman, and I know about women. I'm telling you, that redhead has eyes for you, and—"

"Sheriff! Sheriff!" came a shout from the front of the restaurant.

Packard turned to look as a man dashed to his table, gasping, "There's trouble at the Wild West Saloon! A couple of greenhorn gunslingers are about to shoot it out!"

Getting to his feet, Packard picked up his hat from the chair next to him and put it on. He looked at Monica and sighed. "Sorry, honey. I've got to go. Trouble. You understand."

"I'll walk myself home," she told him coolly, her expression stony.

The lawman was about to remind her she had better get used to such interruptions, then thought better of it and dashed out of the restaurant.

Packard was within twenty yards of the Wild West Saloon when he heard a loud voice from inside shout, "Draw, you coward!" Just before the lawman reached the batwings, a gun roared. Without breaking stride, Packard bolted through the swinging doors to find the victor of the shoot-out standing over his dead opponent, a smoking revolver in his hand. Both men were barely over twenty, and neither man was familiar.

The victor eyed the badge on Packard's chest and explained defensively, "He called me a coward and went for his gun, Sheriff. I didn't have any choice. I had to kill him. Ask any of these men."

Packard looked around at the other customers, many of whom he knew. "What about it, fellas?"

"It was a fair fight, Jess," one of the townsmen answered. "He's telling the truth."

Fixing the gunfighter with a steady gaze, Packard asked, "What's your name, fella?"

"Rick Munson," came the reply.

"Okay, Munson," Packard said flatly, "find your horse and get out of town."

Munson's face flushed angrily, and his mouth tightened. "Hey, what're you talkin' about? You just heard it was a fair fight!"

"You have a hearing problem, mister?" Packard rasped. "I said find your horse and ride."

Munson's expression turned malevolent. Swearing at Packard, he demanded, "Why do I have to leave town when I killed this guy in a fair fight?"

Rubbed raw by the greenhorn's arrogance, the lawman snapped, "Because there's enough trouble and bloodshed in this town without itchy-fingered gunslingers hanging around. Now, do like I said and vamoose."

Sneering, Munson crowed, "So you know I'm a gun-fighter, eh? Heard my name?"

"Nope. You just have that look about you, and you're wearing your Colt halfway to your knees. I've seen your kind a thousand times. Most of you don't last past three shoot-outs."

Clearly growing more cocksure by the second, Rick Munson declared, "I'm not like the rest of them fools. Matter of fact, I'm more than a match for the famous sheriff of Esmeralda County." Holstering his gun, he set his jaw and ordered, "Go for your gun, Packard."

Packard's brown eyes narrowed menacingly. "I've already got a bellyful of you, Munson. You've got three seconds to hit that door."

Munson did not move. A tomblike silence settled over the saloon, and everyone stood as if they were holding their breath. Suddenly the young gunslinger's hand swept downward, his thumb snapping the hammer back with professional accuracy before his fingers had even begun to close around the butt.

That was as far as he would ever get.

Packard's Colt .45 belched flame with a deafening roar, and Munson's body lurched backward. He stumbled over the man he had killed only moments before and crumpled to the sawdust floor, still and lifeless, with a slug in his heart.

Packard broke his gun open, punched out the spent shell, and replaced it with a live one from his gun belt. The haze of gun smoke had not yet cleared when the batwings swung open and Deputy Lee Austin burst through. Pausing only momentarily to look at the bodies on the floor, Austin exclaimed, "Sheriff, we've got a problem at the Golden Nugget! That big Jocko Bane from the Young America has just beaten up Burt Calder, one of the Winnemucca miners. A fight is about to erupt between Troop's hired guns and Uzelac's hired guns!"

Packard shoved his gun into its holster and muttered, "Let's go."

Reaching the Golden Nugget Saloon minutes later, Packard shoved open the swinging doors with Austin on his heels and saw a bloodied, unconscious Burt Calder lying on the floor. The mountain-sized Bane stood over him, glowering at the Winnemucca men sitting at tables nearby and bellowing, "Who's next? You Uzelac boys can talk tough, but let's see how tough you really are! Come on! One of you yellowbellies step up and fight me!"

"That's enough, Bane!" Packard loudly commanded. Looking around the saloon, he was stunned to see his brother sitting at a poker table with Vince Denning, Mel Blanford, and Judd Colden. Alex's face paled under the withering glare of his lawman brother.

The giant silently watched as the lawman knelt beside the unconscious miner and said to the other patrons, "Somebody go get Doc Wren."

Two men hurried out the door, leaving the batwings to swing freely on creaky hinges.

Shaking his head angrily, the sheriff rose to his feet and faced the hulking giant with naked fury. "Just like I thought," he snarled. "You blood-hungry buzzards aren't in town a whole day before this kind of thing happens."

"I couldn't help it, Sheriff," Bane grumbled defensively. "Calder started it."

"That's a lie!" bellowed one of the Winnemucca men.

"That's right, Jess," spoke up another. "Bane came in here just stormin' for a fight. When he started shovin' Burt around, Burt stood up to him. I guess nobody's supposed to do that, so Bane calls it startin' a fight."

Bane rolled his massive shoulders, pointed at the

patron, and roared, "That's your version of it, mister! You want to fight me next?"

"Get out of here, Bane!" commanded Packard, gesturing toward the door. "You'll be billed tomorrow for the doctor's fee for patching up Burt."

The huge man bristled and lashed back, "I told you, Calder started the fight! So I ain't payin' no doctor's fee . . . and I ain't leavin' this saloon till I'm ready! You got that?"

Packard stiffened, and Lee Austin stepped up beside him, saying, "I'll help you, Sheriff."

Patting the deputy's shoulder, Packard said, "Thanks, Lee, but I can handle Goliath."

The huge outlaw swore at Packard and abruptly started after him. Sidestepping adeptly, the sheriff whipped out his revolver and cracked Bane savagely on the temple with the butt, and the giant collapsed, unconscious. The lawman immediately cuffed Bane's hands behind his back, then told Austin to drag him to the jail and lock him up.

Judd Colden leapt to his feet, protesting, "Wait a minute, Sheriff! Why does Jocko have to go to jail?"

"Take a look at Calder."

"But Calder started it!" protested the gang leader.

"You don't really expect me to believe that, do you?" Packard asked incredulously. "Your cohort is twice this man's size. It's this simple: Bane is going to jail, and if he willingly pays Calder's doctor bill tomorrow, I'll let him out. If he balks, he can rot in the cell as far as I'm concerned."

Colden ran a hand to the back of his neck. "Okay, okay," he said, giving in to the sheriff's edict. "Jocko will take care of the bill in the mornin'. Tell him I said he should pay it."

At that moment, Dr. Jacob Wren came in, led by the messengers, and hurried toward the sheriff. Holding his black bag, he looked at the two men on the floor, then at Packard. "Jess, I was told there was only one man down."

"There was when I sent for you, Doc. Never mind the big guy. Take care of Burt."

"Hold on!" blurted Colden. "Jocko's hurt even worse! Look at that gash you put in his head!"

Stepping so close to Colden that their faces were but inches apart, Packard snapped, "Your friend will wake up with nothing worse than a headache. He pounded Burt Calder to a bloody pulp!"

Colden started to speak, then apparently thought the better of it, and Packard turned back to the physician. "Drop your bill by the jail, Doc. I'll see that it gets paid."

With the help of another man, Lee Austin dragged the huge man out of the saloon by the heels, and when they were gone, Packard looked around, making sure all tempers were cooled. Satisfied that the trouble was over for the night, he shot a cold glance at Alex and left. He was about to head back to the office, then decided to wait for a while, hoping that his brother would soon leave as well.

Several minutes later Alex came out of the batwings and did not appear surprised to find his older sibling waiting for him. "I kind of expected to find you here," he remarked dryly. "Actually, I was hoping you'd wait so we can have a talk."

Detaching himself from the wall he had been leaning against, Packard responded softly, "Looks like we need to, little brother. I'm just a bit puzzled, finding you in the company of those thugs."

"I could tell you were upset, seeing me there, but there's really no need to be."

The lawman's eyebrows arched. "No need to be upset when I see my kid brother consorting with killers?"

Alex showed a hint of his temper. "Hey, I wasn't doing anything wrong! I was sitting in on a poker game and catching up on old times with Vince Denning, that's all. We go back a long ways, Jess. When we were kids, we spent a lot of time together. You can't just erase what's in the past. What's wrong with going over some old memories together?"

"Nothing in itself, Alex," the older Packard replied, "but how's it going to look to the townspeople to see you hanging out with a bunch of cutthroats? What's your boss going to think? And more important, what's Lola going to think?"

Alex sighed and said, "Mr. Wood knows me, Jess. He's not going to think I'm turning outlaw. And Lola? Come on, now. It'd take a whole lot more than my spending a little time with Vince for her to question my character. I think you're overreacting, big brother."

"I don't think so," the sheriff parried, "but if I am, it's because I care what happens to you and your family."

Alex laid a hand on his taller brother's arm. "Jess, you've got to understand that Vince and I were once best friends. We were inseparable for a long time. Believe me, I wish he hadn't hooked up with Judd Colden—but knowing him and spending some time with him doesn't make *me* a criminal."

"It could in the eyes of some people, Alex," Packard said evenly. Walking away, he added over his shoulder, "Like I told you this morning, be careful."

Chapter Eight

At sunrise the next morning, Sheriff Jess Packard entered his office and went directly to the cellblock. He glanced at Hugo Stern, who lay on his bunk, staring up at the ceiling, and tried to imagine what the man must be thinking in the few minutes left before his execution.

Shaking his head, he stepped past Stern's cell to Jocko Bane's. The giant was on his feet, gripping the bars of his cell door and obviously waiting for Packard to appear, and he glared at the lawman with hate-filled eyes. Approaching the bars, Packard asked, "Do you remember what I told you last night after you woke up here in your cell? That your boss insists you pay the doctor's fee for what you did to that miner?"

Putting his fingertips gingerly to the knot on his head, Bane grumbled, "Yeah, I remember. And I owe you for *this*, too."

"Maybe so, but I don't advise trying to pay me back," Packard warned.

Bane did not respond. After a few seconds, he muttered, "How much is the fee?"

"Doc Wren said he'd go easy on you. Twenty-five dollars."

"Twenty-five dollars? That's outrageous!"

"That's the fee. Now, are you gonna pay it, or do you want to stay in my jail?"

His face livid with anger, the giant growled, "I hate your guts, Packard!"

"How you feel about me doesn't concern me," the sheriff countered without emotion. "The fee?"

"I'll pay it," muttered the huge man, reaching into his pocket. Thrusting his hands through the bars, he counted out twenty-five dollars in gold pieces on Packard's hand.

Smiling with satisfaction, Packard started unlocking the door just as footsteps sounded in the office. As the sheriff swung the door open, Deputies Ed Murdock, Lee Austin, and Neil Thurston entered the cellblock.

"Okay, Bane, get your carcass out of here," Packard ordered.

Stepping through the door, the giant demanded, "Give me my gun back."

"Deputy Murdock will walk you to the office and give it to you. But let me offer a word of caution: If I have to jail you again, I'm throwing away the key. You'd best walk a straight line, mister."

With Ed Murdock following closely behind him, Bane stomped past the sheriff without comment. Packard then looked at his other deputies and directed them, "Cuff Hugo Stern, fellas. It's time."

The killer was ushered out of the jail and along Pine Street by the sheriff, with the other deputies flanking him. His hands shackled behind his back, Hugo Stern walked unsteadily toward the rising sun.

Aurora's hanging tree was at the east end of Pine Street, where the town butted up against a rise of hills. The centuries-old elm stood tall and sturdy, its massive, bottom-most limb jutting out from the thick trunk eleven feet from the ground. Directly under the tree stood a wagon, its brake set, that was hitched to a team of nervously shifting horses. Just above the wagon bed, a rope dangled from the limb, ending in a hangman's noose.

A large crowd composed of townspeople, miners, and Indians—among them, Joaquin Jim—was in attendance. Judd Colden, his gang, and Virgil Troop and a handful of his miners stood on one side of the tree, while beyond the wagon, on the other side of the tree, stood Art Uzelac, along with his six hired guns and several miners.

When the lawmen and their prisoner drew up to the wagon, the crowd pressed closer. Packard saw his brother standing beside Derek Wood and nodded solemnly to them.

Jess Packard's voice cut the still morning air. "All right, Deputies, hoist the condemned man into the wagon." Hugo Stern suddenly broke into a cold sweat. A pitiful whimper issued from his mouth, and he began quivering all over.

Lee Austin climbed onto the wagon seat while Murdock and Thurston took hold of the trembling prisoner and planted him in the middle of the wagon bed, directly under the noose. Stern stared up at the rope, seemingly unable to tear his eyes away from the instrument of his death.

Hopping into the wagon bed as his deputies alighted, Packard noticed Judd Colden sneering at the Indians and heard his derogatory slur about them to his men. It was evident that Colden hated redmen. Looking away from the outlaw, Packard ran his gaze over the crowd and raised his hands for silence.

When the murmur had died down, the lawman spoke forcefully to the onlookers. "I want all of you to listen to what I have to say. My deputies and I represent the law in Esmeralda County, and one of those laws prohibits the taking of human life in cold blood. Hugo Stern has been duly tried and convicted of three murders committed right here in our town, and one of those victims was a lawman."

Packard let his last words float on the air for a few moments. After the brief pause, he continued. "No one life is any more important than another. However, when Stern took the life of Al Cunningham—whose deputy sheriff's badge was not only an emblem of authority but a symbol of his job as a protector of the law-abiding citizens of this county—when Stern plunged that knife into Deputy Cunningham's chest, he was stabbing every one of you, for the law represents the people. This kind of reckless bloodshed cannot and will not be tolerated in Esmeralda County!"

There was an instant roar of approval from the majority of the crowd, with the notable exceptions of Troop, Uzelac, and their hired guns, who stood silently eyeing each other with granite-like faces.

Proceeding, the sheriff said, "I make this vow to all of you: I will deal harshly with all troublemakers—and especially those who would dare harm my deputies!"

Again the crowd responded eagerly.

Running his hard gaze over the faces of the Troop and Uzelac groups, the lawman concluded, "A potential powder keg is brewing between the Young America and the Winnemucca mines—and the execution that is about to take place is a product of that trouble. I'm warning you men on both sides of the conflict that if any more killing takes place, the guilty parties will end up exactly as Hugo Stern has: facing the noose. Settle your claims dispute in a court of law, not by violence, or you will be dealt with swiftly and severely!"

While the cheers of the crowd continued unabated, Packard turned to his prisoner and asked, "Is there anything you wish to say before we proceed with the execution?"

Stern burst into piteous sobbing, screaming, "Please! Please, Sheriff! Don't kill me! Have mercy! Please!"

Packard eyed him coldly and replied, "Murderers get no mercy from me." With that, he reached up, grasped the noose, and slipped it over Stern's head. Cinching the noose tightly around the killer's neck, the lawman remarked coldly, "I doubt God will have any mercy on you either." Pivoting, Packard hopped over the side of the wagon.

Hugo Stern let loose with a bloodcurdling scream. Raising his voice to be heard above the wailing, Packard looked at his deputy sitting on the wagon's front seat and directed, "All right, Lee."

Austin nodded and snapped the reins, shouting, "Heeyahhh!"

The team bolted forward and jerked the wagon out from under the prisoner's feet, dropping him suddenly. The rope went taut, breaking Stern's neck, and for a few horrible seconds he kicked and spasmed, but then he went still.

As the crowd began to disperse, Joaquin Jim walked over to the sheriff. Packard was aware that Colden was watching him and the Paiute intently as the chieftain remarked, "Sheriff Packard, you are to be commended for your hard hand on criminals. Within my tribe, lawbreakers are similarly dealt with."

Packard nodded. "Unfortunately, sometimes harsh measures are the only ones we can use."

The two shook hands, and Joaquin Jim took his braves and rode away. As the lawman started back toward his office, he glanced over to see Colden still staring at him—and the look on the outlaw's face was anything but admiring.

Four days later, a small caravan of Young America wagons traveled through the Nevada hills, returning from Carson City after delivering ore to the smeltering plants there. Jocko Bane, Mel Blanford, Gene Ortiz, and George Locke were on horseback, acting as guards.

The caravan was within six or seven miles from Aurora when it rolled over a sharp rise, then descended into a draw. Nearing the bottom, Bane spotted two young Paiute braves some thirty yards to his right, standing over a large buck they had just killed with arrows. The giant raised a hand to halt the wagons, then directed Ortiz to stay there while he, Blanford, and Locke quickly rode to the Paiutes.

The Paiutes, who stood silently watching as the three white men approached, were no more than twenty years old and they gripped their bows tightly as the outlaws dismounted. Bane hated Indians as much as his boss did, and when he stepped close to them with Locke and Blanford flanking him, he grinned wickedly. Giving the young braves a stern look, Bane demanded, "You Injuns understand English?"

Both nodded.

"Good! Then you'll understand when I say we're takin' that deer for ourselves."

The taller, huskier brave bristled at Bane's words and protested, "You must not do this, white man. Tando and I have hunted and killed this deer to help feed our people. You have no right to take it from us."

Bane guffawed. "You're redskins. You're the ones who ain't got no rights! We've all the right in the world! This land belongs to us whites."

The smaller youth turned to his friend and said fearfully, "Numaga, it is best if we don't anger these men."

Numaga stiffened, and his expression grew stubborn. "We killed the deer, Tando. It is ours to take to the village. If these white men harmed us, they would have to answer to Joaquin Jim—and I do not think they would want that."

But Bane whipped out his gun and cocked it, pointing it between Numaga's eyes. "I said *we* are takin' the deer, kid!"

George Locke blurted, "Jocko, no! A shot could bring a whole horde of 'em down on us!"

After a long long tense moment, Bane chuckled and said, "Yeah, George, you're right. No gunfire. Instead, I'll just show these filthy red pigs what I think of their kind. You guys hold the little one while I work this one over."

Blanford and Ortiz grabbed Tando and held him fast, and the giant snatched the bow from Numaga's hands, tossing it toward some bushes. Facing the youth, he slapped his face, then punched him square on the jaw. The Indian fell onto his back, and the huge outlaw laughed and kicked him savagely in the face. Then Bane raised his heavy foot and brought it down violently, mashing the youth's nose with his heel. Numaga screamed, then passed out.

Grinning maliciously, the giant turned and glared hatefully at Tando. "You're next, redskin rat!" he growled, lumbering toward him.

Held fast by Bane's cohorts, Tando struggled uselessly. The massive man doubled him over with a punch to the stomach, and the Indian cried out in agony, straining against the hands that held him.

"Let go of him!" bawled the giant. When Tando's arms were released, Bane slammed his fists down on the back of the youth's neck. He fell facedown in the dirt, moaning, then rolled onto his side. Bane laughed with pleasure and kicked him in the face repeatedly until the youth was unconscious.

"Okay, boys," Bane said, enjoying the sight of the Indians lying sprawled on the ground, "let's take the deer and go."

The young braves came to as the caravan rolled out of the draw. Severely battered, their faces bleeding profusely, they struggled to their feet. Numaga mumbled, "We must tell Joaquin Jim what has happened."

With effort, the Paiute youths mounted their ponies. Then leaning on their pintos' necks and holding on to their manes, they headed across the sandy hills toward their village. A short time later, they rode into the village, and their fellow Paiutes gathered around them as the ponies came to a standstill.

Soon Joaquin Jim appeared, drawn by the raised, angry voices of his people. The youths had been laid on the ground by their fathers, and their mothers were coming from their respective wickiups, carrying water and cloths to bathe their sons' battered faces.

Taking one look at them, Joaquin Jim knew without asking what had happened. The chieftain knelt beside the young braves and asked, "What white men did this to you?"

Numaga and Tando described the mountain-sized man who beat and kicked them and the men who were with him. When they mentioned the wagons, Joaquin Jim knew they had to be miners from Aurora.

His voice cold with fury, Numaga's father declared, "They will pay for what they have done!"

Tando's father agreed, adding, "This means war, Joaquin Jim! All the white miners must die!"

The chieftain's wrath was evident in his blazing black eyes, and his muscular chest heaved as he said, "Yes, the miners will pay for what they have done—but let us not declare war until we are forced to, for some of our braves would also wish to stop bullets."

Tando's mother rose to her feet and faced the chieftain. "This talk of war and revenge will not help my son. What will help him is the work of the white medicine man in Aurora."

"The same is true for my son," Numaga's mother interjected.

A babel of voices filled the village, some arguing for war and some against. Joaquin Jim raised his hands for attention, and silence came quickly. Looking around at his people's faces, he told them, "There can be no action taken against the men who did this until Sheriff Jess Packard knows what has happened. In our treaty we agreed that if whites or Paiutes committed crimes against each other, the guilty men would be punished by their own people. However, if the guilty parties are not swiftly punished by Sheriff Packard, we will then put on war paint."

Jess Packard was sitting at his desk in his office, catching up on his mail and enjoying the breeze that swept in through the open door and windows. Hearing footsteps, he looked up to see Lola Packard standing in the doorway, silhouetted against the glare of the sunstruck street.

"Jess, may I see you?" she asked softly.

Rising behind the desk, the tall lawman smiled and said, "Sure. It's always a pleasure to see my beautiful sister-in-law. Come in." Gesturing at the chair in front of the desk, he offered, "Please, sit down."

As she drew closer, Packard could read the worry in her eyes, and when she was across from him, he peered at her and asked, "What's wrong?"

Tears filled Lola's eyes, and she answered, "I deliberately left the children with a neighbor so I could talk with you in private." Throwing a quick look over her shoulder, she queried, "There's no one else here, is there?"

"Nope. We're completely alone," he assured her, sitting down and leaning his elbows on the desk top. "Now, tell me what's bothering you."

"It's Alex," she said, and her lips started trembling. "He's . . . he's spending a lot of time with that outlaw friend of his."

"Vince Denning."

"Vince Denning," she echoed, nodding. "I'm deeply concerned about it, Jess. And I'm not the only one. Derek Wood has spoken to me about it."

"Well, you're looking at someone else who's concerned about it," the lawman remarked. "I had a talk with Alex a few days ago, as a matter of fact, and he got a bit indignant. He told me that he and Vince were once best friends, and that they were only catching up on old times."

"That was what he said to me when I asked him. He acted as though it shouldn't be bothering me—but it does." Wiping away the tears that threatened to spill down her cheeks, Lola asked, "Jess, will you talk to Alex again? He loves you and respects you more than any man. If he's going to listen to anyone, it'll be you."

"Of course I will," Packard promised. "As soon as I can."

Lola thanked him and stood up, and the lawman walked her to the door. Kissing her brother-in-law on the cheek, she left the office.

Not one for putting off something that needed to be done, Packard immediately donned his hat, stepped out onto the boardwalk, and headed for the *Aurora Times* building. When he entered the office, he was welcomed warmly by Monica but less so by her father. Dismissing Derek Wood's coolness as preoccupation with his paper, he said to the publisher, "I see that my brother is busy at the printing press, but I wonder, sir, if Alex could have a few minutes off. I need to talk to him."

When Wood mumbled his permission, Packard went to Alex, telling him they were going to take a little walk, and ushered him out the door. As they made their way along the street, Alex scratched his sandy hair in puzzlement and asked, "What's up? You're not acting like there's an emergency or anything, so what's so important that you got me off from work?"

"To put something to you straight, Alex," the older Packard responded. "You've got to curtail your evenings spent with Denning."

Stopping short, Alex looked his brother in the eye and protested, "But I'm not doing anything wrong! You may be older than me, but that doesn't give you the right to butt into my private life. Vince did a lot for me when we were teenagers in Kansas, and I can't just cut him off. Besides," he added with a grin, "I'm learning to play poker, and I've done quite well in winning."

The lawman shook his head. "You can call it butting in if you want to, but it's not just me who's worried about this situation. Lola came to see me at the office to tell me you've got her upset—and she told me that Derek Wood has discussed the matter with her."

Alex sighed and rubbed the back of his neck. "Jess, I'm sorry for causing Lola undue concern. I sure haven't meant to do that. And I haven't meant to upset Mr. Wood or you for that matter. Okay, I'll cut down the time I spend with Vince, but I won't turn away from him completely. After all, if you're a person's friend, you'll *always* be his friend."

Putting his arm around his older brother's shoulder, Alex remarked, "I'm glad we got these few minutes to talk. Actually, I was going to look you up later and see if we could go hunting together. You know, take a whole day and catch us some venison steaks while they're still on the hoof."

Pleased at his brother's decision about Denning and eager to spend time with Alex, Packard smiled broadly and replied, "I'd really like that. When would you want to do it?"

"How about tomorrow? I've got a little time coming for extra hours I've put in, and tomorrow's the slowest day of the week at the paper, so it'd be the best day for me to take off."

"Then tomorrow it is," the lawman agreed. "I'll be at your house at sunrise."

Leaving Alex at the newspaper office, the sheriff went to see Lola. The children were happily playing in the front yard, and Lola took Packard inside so they could talk undisturbed. As they sat down in the parlor, the lawman told her, "I just talked to Alex, and though he said he can't completely sever his ties with Denning, he'll curtail the time he spends with him." He patted her hand, adding, "And we're going hunting tomorrow, which is Alex's idea."

Smiling wanly, Lola remarked, "I'm glad to know that his connection with Denning hasn't cut him off from you. But I just don't know why his friendship with that man has such a grip on him." Her face suddenly revealed deeper concern, and she said, "This is difficult for me to tell you, but Alex seems to have a lot of money to spend lately, and . . . well, I'm wondering if he and Denning have something shady going."

"Don't lose faith in him completely, Lola," the sheriff advised, standing up to leave. "He told me he's been learning to play poker, and that he's winning a lot."

Brushing a lock of dark hair from her eyes, Lola responded in a worry-filled voice, "You know I love Alex with all my heart, Jess, but I have to confess that this whole thing with Denning has indeed shaken my faith in him. He told me the same thing when I asked where he was getting all this extra cash . . . but I'm not sure he's telling me the truth."

Packard squeezed her shoulder reassuringly and saw himself out. As he walked back toward Pine Street he began having his own doubts about his brother. Absently tugging on his mustache, he asked himself if maybe there *was* more to the "friendship" than met the eye. Shaking his head, he scolded himself for allowing such doubts to enter his mind.

Standing at the counter, Monica Wood finished taking a customer's order for advertising space in the *Aurora Times*, then carried it to Alex Packard, who was working at a layout table at the rear of the office. "More business," she said as she laid the papers on the table.

Smiling broadly, Alex said cheerfully, "Good. That's what we're here for. I'll get right to work on it."

Monica smiled back at him, thinking she had not seen him this cheerful since Vince Denning had come to town. Turning around, she walked to her father's private office at the front of the building and entered after tapping on the door.

Derek Wood looked up from his desk and asked, "Did we get a large advertisement from the clothing store?"

"We sure did. A quarter page. Alex is laying it out right now." Pausing briefly, she added, "He seems more relaxed, now that Jess has talked to him. I guess everything's been straightened out."

Shaking his head slowly, the publisher responded, "I wouldn't be too sure of that, honey. I didn't want to say anything to you about it, but maybe it's best that I do."

"What are you talking about?" Monica queried, feeling concern as she looked down at her father.

Wood hesitated a moment, then answered, "Well, when I had lunch a while ago with some of the merchants, several of them said they had doubts about the Packard brothers."

"Both brothers?" she asked, astonished.

"Yes. There's talk going around town that despite what Alex says about merely catching up on lost time with an old friend, he's actually in cahoots with the Colden gang . . . and perhaps his lawman brother is deliberately turning a blind eye."

Monica's eyes widened. "How could anyone think Jess would be a party to anything shady? Why, that's preposterous!"

Holding up a hand, Wood countered, "Now, honey, you'd best face the fact that your handsome fiancé is made out of flesh, and maybe his salary isn't enough to keep him satisfied. If Alex has something going with those outlaws, it'll mean money in his pocket, and Jess might just be getting some of that money under the table to look the other way." The publisher's voice hardened, and he added, "If that's the case, Jess Packard's sterling reputation—as well as his career—may be badly tarnished."

Monica's face paled. "Father, what are you implying?"

His face stern, Wood replied, "Our family holds a respected place in this community, and our standing would be jeopardized by having a lawman of questionable character as a son-in-law and husband. I certainly hope that should it be necessary to make a decision about Jess, you will consider these factors as well as your feelings."

Chapter Nine

Sheriff Jess Packard was striding up Pine Street toward his office when he came upon a cluster of townsmen who were gathered on the boardwalk in front of the Wild West Saloon.

"Good afternoon, gentlemen," Packard said with a smile, intending to step around them and continue on.

"Say, Sheriff . . .," Gus Widner, the middle-aged owner of the Wild West and two other saloons in Aurora, spoke up.

Halting, Packard asked, "Yeah, Gus?"

"We were just talking about this situation with your brother, and . . . well, I may just as well be frank with you. We don't like the way he's cozying up to the Colder gang."

Not wanting to reveal his own concern over the matter, the lawman replied, "There's something you all need to understand, gentlemen. Vince Denning is simply a boyhood friend of my brother's. You all know Alex. Have you ever had reason to question his character before?"

The men looked around at each other. Shaking his head, Widner replied for the others, "Nope, we sure haven't."

"Well, remember that, will you? My little brother's a sentimental person, and he's just enjoying having someone to share memories of his childhood with. Can you understand that?"

A rumble of voices assured the sheriff that they did, and the saloonkeeper added, "If you tell us that's all it is, we're willing to accept it, Jess. You have our complete confidence."

"Thank you, gentlemen," Packard said, and started on his way.

He stopped suddenly at the sight of a band of a dozen Paiutes, all of them carrying rifles, riding down the street. Led by Joaquin Jim, they were pulling two travois bearing an injured youth on each, and the Indians' faces were hard with fury.

Packard stepped into the street to intercept the chieftain and his braves. One look at the battered young Paiutes told the lawman that they were in bad shape. Raising a friendly hand, the lawman inquired, "Joaquin Jim, what happened?"

"We must get these braves to your medicine man, Sheriff Packard," the chieftain replied with urgency in his voice. "They are hurt very bad."

"I'll take you there," Packard stated. He led them quickly to Jacob Wren's office.

When Numaga and Tando had been admitted to the clinic and were being tended by Dr. Wren and his wife, the lawman and the Indians returned to the street to wait. Facing the chieftain, Packard noted, "Joaquin Jim, I can see that you're angry. Tell me how this happened to your young braves."

The Paiute, his voice bitter, explained what had taken place in the draw a few miles outside of town. Quoting the youths, he described the men who accosted them and stole their deer—in particular, the huge man who had beaten them so savagely. Concluding, he demanded, "By the agreement of our treaty, you must punish the

big white man for what he has done—and you are also
to retrieve the deer."

Anger boiled within Packard toward Judd Colden's
men, especially Jocko Bane. Looking intently into
Joaquin Jim's black eyes, he promised, "You will see
justice done, my friend. We will go to the Young
America mine right now and confront the men who are
responsible."

Getting his horse, Packard led the band of Indians
out of Aurora, and within minutes they were nearing
the mine. When the sheriff and the Paiutes got within
sight of the mine office, Packard could see Judd Colden
and Vince Denning sitting on the porch. By the time
the riders reached the building, Virgil Troop was standing in front of the porch, waiting for them, flanked by
Colden and Denning.

Instructing Joaquin Jim and his braves to remain
on their pintos, Packard dismounted. The lawman
ignored the hate-filled glares of the white men and
stepped close to Troop. Without preamble, Packard
announced, "On the way back from Carson City,
Colden's pal Jocko Bane beat two young Paiutes to a
bloody pulp and stole their deer, then left the boys
lying unconscious."

Colden bristled and demanded, "How do you know
them Indians ain't lyin'?"

Packard's muscular body seemed to swell with his
anger. "Because they'd never seen your men before,
but they described them perfectly—especially Bane."

"Aw, maybe they *had* seen 'em and just wanted to
stir up trouble, so they made it all up."

Packard strode to the porch and eyed the gang leader.
His face darkening with rage, he growled, "Doc Wren
is stitching them up this minute—and believe me, they
didn't make up their gashes and bruises! Besides, all we

have to do is find your men. If they've got a big buck, we'll know where they got it."

Virgil Troop's expression changed from indignation to contrition, and it was obvious that he had already seen the deer. Rubbing his chin, he was clearly uncomfortable as he said, "Sheriff, I'm really sorry that this has happened."

Packard assessed the mineowner. Troop was upset, all right, but the sheriff figured it had far less to do with the fact that two innocent Indian youths had been severely beaten than because attention had been drawn to the hired guns. The lawman asked harshly, "Do you know where those scum are right now?"

Pointing toward the big house, just visible through the trees, Troop replied, "That's where they live."

The lawman studied the place for a moment, then ordered, "You three are coming with us to see if they've got the deer."

Troop, Colden, and Denning reluctantly accompanied the sheriff and the Paiutes down the gentle, shady slope to the big house. As they drew near, voices punctuated with laughter came from the rear of the house. Rounding the corner, they came upon the four outlaws standing beside the carcass of the deer, which was hanging by its heels from the limb of a tall cottonwood. Jocko Bane and George Locke, their hands bloodied, were gutting it, while Mel Blanford and Gene Ortiz watched.

The outlaws seemed almost stunned by the sight of the Indians and the sheriff, and when Joaquin Jim signaled his men to dismount, the foursome stiffened as if ready to fight. Packard swung from his saddle and shot a malevolent glance at Bane, then said to the other three, "You men have violated the law by stealing this deer from the two Paiute braves."

"Look, Sheriff," spoke up Ortiz, "we just—"

"Shut up!" Packard hollered. "Your excuses are worthless! And what's worse," he continued, breathing hotly, "you stood by and let your friend here batter those boys senseless."

"Now, look, Packard," Locke snapped, "Jocko does whatever he wants! Look at the size of him! What could we do to stop him?"

Packard shook his head, and his face was filled with disgust. "You didn't even try to stop him. You encouraged him! You're nothing but yellowbellied cowards for being a party to such a deed."

Turning his fury on Bane, the lawman growled, "And as for you, Bane, you're under arrest for assault and battery. Those men standing beside their chief are the fathers of the boys you brutalized, and they're pressing charges!"

The huge outlaw was stunned. Throwing down the blood-soaked hunting knife in his hands, he swore and said, "Now, just a minute, Sheriff! Indians ain't got no right to press charges against a white man!"

"That's right!" Colden loudly agreed.

Packard stiffened. "Aside from the fact that the Paiutes were on this land long before white men stole it from them, their village is in Esmeralda County, which puts them under the jurisdiction and protection of the sheriff's office," he said coldly. "They have as much right to press charges against white men who commit crimes against them as anyone else. Like I said, Bane, you're under arrest. You'll face trial for these charges, and no doubt you'll go to prison for at least five years."

The hulking giant swore at Packard, shouting, "I ain't goin' to prison for beatin' up stinkin' Indians!" As he spoke, Bane looked over at Colden and Troop, clearly expecting them to back him . . . but there were a dozen armed Paiutes and one tough sheriff to reckon with, and silence prevailed from his bosses.

Packard, too, read the silence, and he growled, "Well, Bane, it looks like your friends aren't prepared to go up against these braves and me. And I assume you have enough sense not to go for your gun, 'cause you'd be dead before you could grip the butt. So are you going to hand over your weapon and come easy-like, or are you going to make it hard on yourself?"

Angered beyond reason, the giant shot a string of curses at the lawman, then abruptly grabbed an ax leaning against the house and swung it forcefully at the sheriff's head. But the agile Packard ducked, and the ax head was buried in a tree.

Bane reacted fast and violently. Breaking the ax handle off at the head, he went after Packard with the club. Again the lawman adeptly dodged the deadly weapon and, catching Bane off balance, drove a vicious blow into the giant's midsection. When Bane doubled over from the punch, Packard slammed him violently on the jaw.

Stumbling backward from the blow, Bane slammed into the hanging carcass of the deer, losing his grip on the ax handle. Packard quickly closed in and cracked Bane with another blow to the jaw, and the massive man was knocked down into the pile of entrails beside the deer.

Bane got to his feet, sticky with blood and boiling with anger, and went after Packard. The giant slammed the lawman hard, but Packard, though winded, recovered.

Grunting from the effort, the two adversaries traded innumerable punches, any one of which would have knocked out most other men. The onlookers stood watching in silent amazement, never taking their eyes from the combatants. Occasionally one of the bystanders winced automatically when a particularly powerful punch found its mark and blood oozed in confirmation.

Although the lawman took several powerful blows to the head and chest, he was tough and fast, and he slowly whittled the bigger man down to size. When Bane began to weaken, Packard spotted the discarded ax handle and picked it up, grasping it with both hands. Planting his feet, the sheriff whacked Bane savagely in the groin, and the huge man doubled over in agony, cursing the lawman.

Packard decided to end the battle. Gripping the ax handle firmly, he swung it with all his might squarely on Jocko Bane's mouth, knocking out both of the giant's front teeth. Bane fell flat on his back, unconscious, while Troop and his hired guns looked on in awe.

For several moments no one moved. Then Joaquin Jim hurriedly conferred with the youths' fathers and stepped beside Packard who was gasping for air. Laying a hand on the lawman's shoulder, the chieftain declared in his deep voice, "You have done justice for our two young braves. We will not press charges if the medicine man's bill is paid, the deer is returned, and the men involved make public apology to Numaga and Tando."

The lawman's having emerged victorious after whittling the huge outlaw down to size seemed to have shaken Virgil Troop, and he promptly volunteered, "Sheriff, I'll pay the doctor bill for the boys and have this deer taken by wagon to the Paiute village." Turning to his henchman, he urged, "And Judd, see that your men make that public apology."

Colden's face reflected his reluctance, but he faced his men and ordered, "You heard Mr. Troop, boys. I don't much cotton to the notion, but we're workin' for him, so you'll make that apology."

Locke opened his mouth to protest, but Colden speared him with a hot look and growled, "No arguments, George!"

Locke glumly responded, "Whatever you say, Judd."

"What's this . . . about an . . . apology?" Jocko Bane suddenly interjected as he came to. Spitting teeth and blood, he struggled to his feet. When Colden explained the situation, Bane roared, "I ain't gonna apologize for nothin'!"

"Then you'll be goin' to jail, Jocko," the gang leader stated. "These redskins got our backs against the wall. There ain't no other way."

Grudgingly, his hand held to his bleeding mouth, he grunted, "Okay, boss. I sure don't hanker goin' to prison."

Marched into town behind a wagon bearing the deer and surrounded by the band of Paiutes, the gang members were taken to the clinic. The Paiute youths, now stitched and bandaged, were escorted out to the street, where the presence of the Troop bunch, the Paiutes, and the sheriff had drawn a sizable crowd.

After briefly telling the onlookers what had happened, Jess Packard turned to the outlaws and said caustically, "And now, *gentlemen*, I believe you have something to say to Numaga and Tando."

Though it clearly galled them, Jocko Bane, George Locke, Mel Blanford, and Gene Ortiz made their apologies to the young braves, and when they had finished, Joaquin Jim stepped to Packard and smiled. "Sheriff Packard, you are a man of your word. Justice has been done."

The chieftain then directed his men to mount up, and the youths were placed once again on the travois.

When the Indians and the wagon were gone, Packard glared at Colden and his men and told them, "I hope this is the last trouble I'm going to have from you."

No one said anything in reply.

His dark eyes boring into the men, Packard tugged on his mustache and warned, "If you still aren't convinced that it'll cost you to break the law in this county, you'd better think twice. There are probably other places where you can run roughshod over the people and the law, and if that's what you're after, find your horses and hightail it out of Esmeralda County." With that, he turned on his heel and walked off.

Staring after the retreating lawman with a diabolical hatred, Judd Colden was enraged by Packard's threats and actions against his men and told himself that the sheriff had to be eliminated. He called to his men to return to the mine, and as he headed back with the others, he said nothing about killing Packard. He would have to think about it further, for Packard would certainly not be easy to kill.

The Packard brothers headed into the mountains to hunt at sunrise the next morning, not planning to return before dark. Saying only that he and Alex were going into the Sierras, Sheriff Jess Packard had left his deputies in charge.

At midmorning, when Art Uzelac was standing beside a wagonful of gold ore in front of his office, two of his hired guns emerged from the nearby bunkhouse and approached him.

"Me and Ted are gonna walk into town, Mr. Uzelac," Yancey Davis stated. "Anything we can get you?"

"Yeah," the mineowner replied. "Pick me up some pouch tobacco and some paper for the makin's, will you? I'll pay you for it when you get back."

"Will do," Davis promised.

Walking in a leisurely fashion down the hill, Davis and Ted Fowler soon reached the winding road that led into town. They had just strolled into a deeply shaded spot where the road passed through a thick stand of junipers when suddenly a staccato of gunfire came from the dense trees, and both men went down. Fowler was killed instantly, but Davis, though hit three or four times, was still alive and conscious. Desperately clawing for his gun, he pulled it out and was attempting to shoot back when three more shots rang out, and Yancey Davis collapsed and went still.

Deputy Lee Austin was in the cellblock, sweeping the floor, when he heard heavy footsteps in the office. An angry voice thundered, "Sheriff, you in here?"

Leaning the broom against the wall, Austin hurried into the office to find Art Uzelac and two of his hired strong arms. The mineowner had fire in his eyes. "Where's Packard?" Uzelac loudly demanded.

"He's on a hunting trip," replied the deputy. "Took a much-needed day off. You have a problem?"

"No, I've got *two* problems!" Uzelac snapped. "Come here. I'll show 'em to you!"

Leading Austin outside, he gestured toward a horse that bore two corpses draped over its back. "Yancey Davis and Ted Fowler! Murdered!"

Pushing his hat to the back of his head, Austin asked, "When and where did it happen?"

"About twenty minutes ago. They were walkin' to town from the mine. Some killers were waitin' in that spot where the road bisects that dense stand of trees and shot 'em down without mercy. I don't know who did it, but I know who's responsible. I want Troop and his bunch arrested immediately!"

Austin asked, "Do you have proof that whoever killed these men were among Troop's hirelings?"

"No, I don't, but you and I both know Troop ordered it done!"

Keeping his voice low and level, the deputy responded, "Now, Mr. Uzelac, there'll have to be an investigation. As soon as Sheriff Packard gets back—"

"When are you expectin' him?"

"Well, I don't know for sure. If he gets a deer quickly, he'll more than likely head back right away. If not, he'll probably not show up till sundown or later."

"This can't wait!" bellowed the furious mineowner. "Where'd he go? I'll send some men after him."

"He went into the Sierras."

"Well, that covers a lot of territory," Uzelac noted sarcastically. "Did he go straight west, North, South?"

"I don't know," Austin replied with a sigh.

"Where are the other deputies?"

"They're out patrolling the town."

"I want you to get 'em, and the three of you arrest Troop, Colden, and the rest of those dirty killers!"

"Mr. Uzelac, Sheriff Packard will have to be in charge of this, but I assure you that the minute he returns, the proper steps will be taken."

Swearing profusely, Uzelac smashed a fist into a palm and growled, "Then I'm campin' right here till Packard shows up!"

"Fine," Austin rejoined. He headed out the door to go on his usual patrol.

The day wore on, and it was not until late afternoon that the Packard brothers rode into town with a packhorse bearing a large buck. Advised of the murders by a bystander, Jess Packard told Alex to go home while he rode straight to his office.

As he hauled up next to the horse that still bore the

corpses, Art Uzelac emerged through the office door, followed by his two men. The deputies were on their heels. "Well, finally!" the mineowner roared as the sheriff dismounted. "Seems to me you're bein' paid to uphold the law around here, Packard, not to be off somewhere huntin' deer!"

Not bothering to dignify the man's verbal assault with a reply, Packard eyed the bodies and asked, "What happened?"

"Two of my best men were murdered, that's what happened! I want Virgil Troop, Judd Colden, and the rest of that gang arrested!"

"Now, hold on, Art," Packard said quietly. "Let's have some details."

Uzelac filled the sheriff in on when and where his men had been cut down, then insisted once more that Troop and his strong arms be arrested. "I know they're responsible."

"I'll have to have proof of that," Packard told him. "But I'll go out right now and question Virgil, as well as check the spot where the men were shot. Maybe the killers were careless and left some clues."

"I'm goin' with you," Uzelac stated flatly.

"You can go with me to look for evidence, but when I talk to Troop, I go alone."

Agreeing to Packard's terms, the mineowner told the men with him to take the bodies to the undertaker. Then he mounted up and rode out with the sheriff.

After a thorough search of the area, Packard told Uzelac there were no clues as to who had gunned down his men. Uzelac snorted, "Who needs clues? We both know the killers are among Virgil Troop's hired guns. Now, are you gonna make some arrests?"

"I'm going to the Young America right now," replied Packard. "After I've questioned Troop, I'll come to your place and let you know what's happened."

*   *   *

Dusk was falling when Packard arrived at the Winne-mucca mine. The mineowner sat smoking a cigar on the porch of his cabin near the mouth of the mine, joined by several miners and his four remaining gunmen. Seeing the lawman, Uzelac got to his feet, and when Packard drew up, the burly mineowner stepped off the porch and demanded, "Well?"

"Virgil denies any connection with the killings. So does Judd Colden."

"Well, of course they do! Are you just gonna let 'em get away with it?"

There was strain in Packard's voice as he responded, "Art, you helped me search the spot where your men were murdered. Did you see anything there that would incriminate Troop or his men?"

"No, but that doesn't mean—"

"Look," Packard cut in, "I can't make an arrest based on assumption. I have to have proof. Without proof, my hands are tied."

Uzelac seethed silently. Finally, he snapped, "You shouldn't have left town for a stupid hunting trip with things as they are around here! Troop must have known you were out of town and figured it was the perfect time to order the killings. If you'd have been in Aurora instead of gallivanting up there in the mountains, Davis and Fowler would still be alive!"

The man's words angered Packard more than they stung, and he countered, "I can't blame you for being upset over your men being killed, but to say it wouldn't have happened if I hadn't gone hunting is pushing it pretty far. The killings took place outside of town. What difference would it have made if I had been at my office?"

When Uzelac did not answer, Packard said tightly, "Don't get any ideas about retaliation, Art. You'll only start a war that will soak these hills with blood. And some of it might be your own."

Uzelac still made no reply.

Reining his horse around, Packard reminded him, "Davis and Fowler knew the risks when they took the job as your hired guns—the same as these other fellas here. As sure as the sun rises and sets, more men are going to get killed unless you and Troop settle your dispute in court." Nodding curtly, Packard rode away into the rapidly darkening night.

Chapter Ten

At midmorning the next day, Monica Wood was at the office of the *Aurora Times*, idly looking out the window, when the McGuire buckboard rolled past. Everett and Mamie McGuire were seated in the bed, while Angie McGuire drove the wagon. Muttering to herself, Monica headed swiftly for the door.

Her father, who was dealing with a customer at the counter, called, "Monica! Where are you going?"

The blonde did not reply or even look back at him as she opened the door and hurried outside. Lifting her skirt slightly, Monica ran along the boardwalk, barely dodging people while keeping her gaze fixed on the wagon that she assumed was headed for Jacob Wren's clinic. Monica feared that when the McGuires passed the sheriff's office, Jess Packard would see it and go to greet them—particularly the beautiful redhead.

Monica was so intent on her mission that she did not see a large man coming out of the tobacco shop, and she bumped into him, losing her balance. The man quickly grasped her arm to keep her from falling, and she thanked him perfunctorily, raised her skirt ankle-high once more, and resumed her pace. The buckboard had now passed the sheriff's office and was hauling up in front of the clinic.

Breathing hard by the time she reached the sheriff's

office, the anxious blonde stopped and peered in the window. Her fiancé was not behind the desk, and there was no sign of anyone in the office.

Relieved, Monica continued along the boardwalk at a more leisurely pace and watched as the McGuire women helped Everett from the wagon. When the blonde was within earshot of the clinic, she stopped and, trying to look casual, leaned against a wall in the shade and listened in on the McGuires' conversation.

"Aunt Mamie, while the doctor's examining Uncle Everett, I'll do my shopping at the general store," Angie said as she and her aunt assisted her uncle up the steps of the clinic.

"Good idea, Angie," the older woman responded.

The couple entered the clinic, and Angie turned to cross the street. Monica watched as the redhead threaded her way through the traffic, angling across the broad street toward the general store. Angie's auburn hair caught the sun, which made it gleam like copper, and Monica had to admit to herself that Angie McGuire was indeed a fetching woman. When Angie entered the store, Monica stood there, uncertain as to what to do next.

Suddenly spotting Jess Packard coming out of the gun shop up the street, the blonde stepped to the edge of the boardwalk and waved, calling the lawman's name. He smiled and headed toward her, weaving his way across the thickly trafficked street.

"Hello, darling," Monica said sweetly as he drew up. "I stopped by your office to see you."

"Business or pleasure?" he asked, holding a box of cartridges in the crook of his arm.

"Pleasure, of course," she replied, batting her eyes. "It's always pleasure when I'm with you."

"You do say the nicest things," he remarked, smiling broadly.

Monica realized that facing down the street as he was, her fiancé could easily see the general store, and eager to keep him from seeing Angie when she came out, she pointedly turned so that Packard would have his back to the store. "Alex mentioned that you got a deer yesterday," she said.

The sheriff shifted with her and responded, "Sure did."

Keeping a steady eye on the store over the lawman's shoulder, Monica murmured, "Alex didn't say which one of you actually shot it—but I'll bet it was you."

"Actually, we both did," he said, chuckling. "It probably wouldn't happen again in a hundred years. We both saw the deer at the same time and squeezed the triggers simultaneously. A split second before my gun roared, I heard Alex's fire. One thing's for sure—that ol' buck didn't have a chance."

Monica giggled, then turned the subject to their new house, all the while keeping the general store in sight. She was in the middle of a sentence when the redhead appeared, carrying a small paper sack.

Angie stepped to the edge of the boardwalk and was about to venture across the street when two of Judd Colden's men—George Locke and Gene Ortiz—came out of a saloon and suddenly stepped in front of her.

Locke leered at her and said, "Well, look who's here!"

Recognizing the outlaw, Angie's face went rigid as she muttered, "Please get out of my way."

Gene Ortiz moved up beside Locke and, ignoring the scornful look he received from the redhead, told her, "Aw, now, honey, it ain't nice to be so rude."

"How dare you call me honey!" Angie snapped. "Please, I asked you to get out of my way."

When Locke did not move, Angie turned and started

around him, but the Mexican quickly blocked her path. Her face reddened, and her lips pressed tight with suppressed fury. When she wheeled toward the boardwalk to escape them, Locke seized her arm. She glared at him, demanding loudly, "Let go of me!" and jerked her arm free.

"You really are a spitfire, aren't you, honey?" Locke remarked with a chuckle, reaching for her.

"Leave me alone!" she shouted.

Hearing the redhead's shout, Packard turned around in time to see Locke roughly grab her. He immediately thrust the box of cartridges into Monica's hands, saying tersely, "Hold this."

Without waiting for a response—or noticing Monica's smoldering anger—the lawman stormed across the street to Angie's rescue.

The sheriff's patience was worn thin by Colden and his men, and seeing the outlaws forcing themselves on the lovely young woman from the way station filled him with rage. "Locke! Ortiz!" Packard snarled. "Let go of her!"

The outlaws' heads whipped around, but Locke maintained his hold on Angie. Glaring at Packard defiantly, Locke retorted, "Mind your own business!"

Packard's dark brown eyes gleamed with his anger. "This *is* my business! I said let go of her!"

"When we're ready, we will—not before," Locke challenged.

Ortiz took a step toward the sheriff. "We've had about as much of you as we can stomach, lawman," he railed, shoving Packard back.

Packard's gun was out in a flash, and he smashed the Mexican on the cheekbone. Blood spurted from the gash as Ortiz collapsed like a rag doll. Going to his friend's defense, Locke released Angie and attempted to kick the gun from Packard's hand, but his foot missed and he landed in the dirt.

Angie immediately backed away, and Packard gave her a quick glance and asked, "Are you all right?"

Rubbing her arms where the outlaws had gripped her, the redhead started to answer when Locke sprang from the ground and tackled Packard. The impact caused the revolver to fly out of the sheriff's hand and out of reach, forcing Packard to grapple with his defiant opponent.

"I'm sick and tired of takin' orders from you, lawman!" Locke snarled.

"Then get out of my county!" countered the sheriff as he locked the outlaw's neck in the crook of his right arm and gripped Locke's wrist with the other hand.

Locke gagged and tried to break free, but his struggle was useless against the strength and ferocity of the lawman. Holding the outlaw tight in the vise-like grip of his arm, the sheriff growled through clenched teeth, "When I told you to let go of Miss McGuire, I meant it! I guess I'll just have to convince you of that!"

Releasing the outlaw's neck, Packard grasped him by the collar and seat of his pants and propelled him headfirst toward the hitch rail. Locke tried desperately to resist, but Packard's arms were unyielding, and he drove Locke's head into the rail, rendering the man unconscious. Blood oozed from a gash on the outlaw's head as Packard dropped his limp form and stood over him, breathing hard.

Looking across the street, he saw Monica staring intently at him, a distinct look of displeasure on her face. He started toward her when he felt a soft hand on his arm, then gazed down into a pair of beautiful blue eyes.

"Thank you, Sheriff, for coming to my rescue," Angie

told him. "I don't know what those filthy beasts would have done to me."

Smiling, Packard responded, "You're more than welcome. It was my duty as a gentleman as well as my duty as sheriff. Are you sure you're all right?"

"I'm fine," she answered, nodding and removing her hand from his arm. Looking around at the spectators, none of whom had come to her aid, she added, "Too bad there aren't more gentlemen in this town."

Shaking his head, Packard remarked, "Well, Aurora's a real tough place. I'm afraid folks see too much of this kind of thing every day." Glancing at Locke and Ortiz, the sheriff said, "You'll have to excuse me now. Much as I'd like to leave these scum lying here bleeding, I suppose I'd better see to them."

The cut on Ortiz's cheek needed stitching, and the deep gash on Locke's head also needed to be sewn up. After getting several men to help him, Packard carted the gang members to the doctor's office.

Angie McGuire trailed along behind the procession, and just as Packard and the others reached the door of the clinic, Everett and Mamie McGuire came out. The redhead told them of being accosted and of the sheriff's coming to her rescue, and the McGuires thanked Packard for taking care of their niece.

While the lawman and his helpers took the outlaws inside, Angie and Mamie assisted Everett into their wagon. The way-station manager had just settled in when Packard emerged from the clinic and walked toward the buckboard.

"Well, it sure does seem like you folks run into a passel of trouble every time you come to Aurora. Maybe you ought to start carrying a lucky charm," he quipped.

Laughing, Angie gazed up at the tall, handsome lawman and rejoined, "What do we need a lucky charm for when we have you?"

Suddenly Monica Wood was standing beside them, glaring at Angie. Her temper flaring, the blonde railed, "You obviously didn't notice me following you, but I've been watching and listening to you, Miss McGuire, and I've had more than enough! Just who do you think you are?"

Clearly shocked, Angie peered at Monica and asked, "Pardon me? Do I know you?"

Fuming, Monica spoke in a loud, shrill voice that attracted the attention of nearly everyone on the street. "I'll tell you who I am! I'm the woman who's engaged to this man you're practically drooling all over!"

Angie's mouth fell open. "What are you talking about?"

"You know what I'm talking about, you hussy!"

Packard stiffened. Glancing at the bystanders, who stood staring at the confrontation, he muttered in an angry voice, "Monica, this is unseemly and uncalled for."

"Uncalled for?" the blonde exploded. "I told you this woman has eyes for you, but you're too blind to see it!" Facing Angie again, she spat, "Jess is *my* man! You leave him alone!"

Keeping his voice low, the lawman declared, "Monica, you have no cause to speak to Miss McGuire this way. She was in trouble, and I helped her. That's my job, in case you've forgotten."

Monica retorted, "Why couldn't you let some other man go to her rescue? I told you the other night that she's got her sights set on you!"

"And I told you that that's all in your imagination," Packard countered, the angry edge in his voice becoming more evident. "And this badge on my chest demands that I protect people from harm, whether they're male or female."

Angie interjected, "Would you have him just stand by and watch someone being mauled or molested and not do something—"

"You shut up!" the indignant blonde shrieked. "I'm on to your wiles. Jess may be blind to them, but I'm not! I know what you are, even if he doesn't! And I'll thank you not to be so familiar with him! The very idea, putting your hand on his arm that way!"

Quietly, the redhead responded, "What you've seen in my eyes when I've looked at your man, Miss Wood, is admiration. Granted, he is a handsome and kind man, but I have no designs on him. He told me a week ago, while my uncle was being treated by Dr. Wren, that he was engaged to you and that you're to be married next month. You can think what you wish, but I'm not trying to take him from you. And as for touching Sheriff Packard, it was only an innocent gesture."

Monica opened her mouth to speak, but Angie cut her off by saying, "I was engaged once, Miss Wood, but the man turned out to be a cad. You should be thankful the sheriff is such a good man." Then, with a slight cutting edge in her voice, she added, "Another thing, Miss Wood. If you love Sheriff Packard, you should never embarrass him . . . especially in public."

Monica stood nonplussed, gritting her teeth. Mamie McGuire quickly filled the silence, telling her niece, "Angie, dear, we need to get back to the way station."

The redhead nodded, gave Monica a frosty look, then said to Packard as she climbed onto the seat, "Thank you, once again, Sheriff, for your help."

Disregarding Monica's wrath, the lawman smiled and replied, "Glad I could be of help."

With a last wave at Packard, Angie snapped the reins and drove away.

When the sheriff turned around, he saw Monica striding stiffly up the street toward the newspaper office. The box of cartridges was on the ground, its contents spilling out and gleaming in the sunlight.

The McGuire wagon was approaching the bottom of Sonora Pass, and sitting in the bed beside her sleeping husband, Mamie McGuire had been silently watching her niece for quite some time. Rising to her knees, Mamie leaned up to the seat and looked at Angie's face. There were tears coursing down the young woman's cheeks.

"Angie, dear," Mamie murmured, "I'm sorry you had to take such abuse from that woman."

Sniffing, the redhead replied, "I don't care about that."

"Then what are you crying about?"

There was a pause, then Angie answered, "He's such a good man, Aunt Mamie, and his fiancée embarrassed him terribly in front of all those people."

Mamie assessed her niece for a moment, then asked, "Is that all you're crying about?"

After a much longer pause Angie glanced over her shoulder and, evading the question, finally responded, "Our talking may wake Uncle Everett, and he needs his rest."

Virgil Troop and Judd Colden were sitting in the Young America office, drinking whiskey, when a miner opened the door. Sticking his head inside, the man announced, "George Locke and the Mexican are comin' back, and they're both all bandaged up!"

Troop and Colden bounded outside, waiting on the

porch as the outlaws rode up. Gene Ortiz was holding a
hand to his bandaged face, while Locke, gauze wrapped
around his head, was bending over and looked dazed.
Troop blurted, "You guys run into a mountain lion?"

Dismounting, Ortiz replied, "I wish it had been a
mountain lion. We might have gotten off lighter. It was
Packard."

Colden exploded, "Packard? Why did he do this?"

"Well, we spotted that cute redhead from the way
station in town and decided to have a little fun. But the
tin star came along and got rough." He shook his head,
then added, "At least he didn't arrest us. He said
somethin' about the injuries bein' enough punishment."
Jerking his thumb toward his partner, he noted, "George
ain't doin' so good. He still ain't come out of it al-
together. The doc said he got a concussion and should
stay in bed for a couple of days."

At that moment Jocko Bane and Mel Blanford appeared at the mouth of the mine. Pointing at their two
injured cronies, they spoke hurriedly to each other,
then strode over. "What happened?" Bane demanded.

Colden briefly explained, then instructed several miners passing by to help the injured men down to the
house. As he watched Locke and Ortiz being led away,
the gang leader's face darkened menacingly. Turning to
Troop, he stated flatly, "It's time to rid Aurora and
Esmeralda County of Sheriff Jess Packard."

"But how?" Troop asked. "Packard's a one-man
army."

"There's gotta be a way," Colden growled. "He ain't
immortal."

"Maybe not, but a whole lot of men have tried to
prove that . . . and every one of 'em's dead," Troop
pointed out.

Bane volunteered, "I'll kill the skunk, Judd. I owe

him plenty. It'll do my heart good to send him outta this world."

Troop scratched his head and said, "You may be big and Packard may be mortal, but he's a hard man to kill. I'm warning you: Be real careful."

"Just how're you gonna do it?" Colden asked. "I don't want you gettin' yourself killed."

The giant laughed. "Don't worry, Judd. I'm gonna shoot the skunk in the back. See, I found out that when the saloons close at midnight, Packard lets his deputies go home, and then he makes his rounds before goin' to his hotel room." He smiled. "So while he's puttin' the town to bed tonight, I'll send him to meet his Maker."

Chapter Eleven

Shortly after midnight, Sheriff Jess Packard began patrolling Aurora's main thoroughfare, which was lit by staggered lamps on both sides of the street, four to a block. Walking from dim shadows to pools of yellow light, the lawman started down the south side of Pine Street, checking the doors of the stores and shops and making sure they were locked. Two drunken miners stood in front of the Golden Nugget Saloon, looking around in bewilderment. Approaching them, Packard eventually determined from their almost incoherent ramblings that they were from the Young America, and he pointed them in the right direction for home and watched them meander off.

The sheriff came to an intersection and started to cross, listening to the sound of his own footsteps echo off the false-fronted clapboard buildings. Packard was halfway across the side street when his lawman's sixth sense made him freeze in his tracks—and then the barely audible sound of a hammer being cocked made him hit the ground.

As he fell flat and whipped out his revolver, a gun roared from the deep shadows directly behind him, and a bullet whizzed just over his head. Packard fired at the flash of light he had seen from the corner of his eye, then heard a grunt. Several seconds later another shot came, but the slug missed Packard by six feet, chewing into the ground. Rolling twice, the sheriff fired again, this time eliciting an agonized cry of pain and the sound of shuffling boots.

Packard sprang to his feet just as Jocko Bane staggered from the blackness of the side street into the light of a streetlamp. The massive outlaw had been hit in the left shoulder, and a bright red furrow showed where one of the sheriff's bullets had plowed across the giant's cheek. Bane focused on the lawman with wild, bulging eyes, cursed and railed threateningly, and then raised his revolver to fire again.

Packard's Colt .45 was cocked and aimed at Bane's chest. "Don't do it!" the lawman warned.

But Bane clearly intended to kill Packard and was about to fire when Packard's weapon roared, sending a slug into the center of the giant's enormous chest. Jolted by the impact, Bane stumbled backward and fell. The gun in his hand discharged, but the bullet went wild.

Cocking his revolver, Packard cautiously walked toward the fallen outlaw, who was flat on his back, gasping for breath. As the lawman approached, Bane struggled to raise his weapon, finally lining the muzzle on the sheriff. Packard again warned the outlaw to put down his weapon, but Bane ignored the lawman and struggled to pull the trigger. Just before Bane fired, Packard sent a bullet ripping into the man's forehead, killing him instantly.

At the big house down the hill from the Young America mine, Judd Colden, Vince Denning, and Mel Blanford sat ringing the large table in the dining room, playing a game of cards, while their two wounded cohorts were in their beds on the second floor. Cigarettes dangled from Colden's and Blanford's mouth, and Denning was nursing a nearly empty whiskey bottle.

Holding his cards in one hand, Blanford pulled a gold watch from his pocket and said, "It's nearly twelve-thirty, Judd. If Jocko was gonna kill Packard, it oughta be done by now."

"He'll show up in a few minutes," Colden said confidently. "Jocko's a born killer. If anyone can get the job done, he can."

Suddenly there was a knock at the front door.

"See, what'd I tell you?" Colden asked, chuckling as he rose and headed toward the door. "Jocko's back with good news."

"If that's Jocko," Denning muttered, "why's he knockin'?"

The cigarette still dangling, Colden answered over his shoulder, "Maybe the door's locked."

Pulling open the door, Colden stared into the face of his massive friend. But Jocko Bane's head lolled to one side, his eyes stared vacantly, a blue hole penetrated his forehead, and a heavy smear of blood decorated the side of his face. The shocked gang leader's mouth sagged open, and the cigarette tumbled from his lips onto the floor, where it lay unnoticed and smoldering.

The other two outlaws had caught sight of their cohort's body filling the doorway and quickly dashed over to flank Colden. Suddenly the huge corpse was thrust through the door, slamming into Colden and falling in a heap. The three outlaws stumbled backward, then stood in stunned silence as Sheriff Jess Packard strode stiffly through the doorway.

Packard stared unwaveringly at the gang leader for a long moment. "It didn't work, Colden," the lawman stated, his voice ragged. "And by the look on your face, you must have thought your henchman could pull it off. Sorry to disappoint you."

Colden labored to hide his shock at his cohort's death

and his disappointment at Packard's survival. "I don't know what you're talkin' about," he finally muttered, his voice sounding hollow.

"Don't try to kid me, you lying snake. You sent Bane to shoot me in the back."

Shaking his head emphatically, Colden protested, "That ain't true, Sheriff!"

"Don't give me that," Packard retorted, sneering. "Bane never blew his nose unless it came as an order from you. *You* wouldn't try to back-shoot me, but you'd gamble your friend's life on it."

"You got it all wrong, Packard," the gang leader said flatly. "Me and the boys here, we didn't know where Jocko was."

"That's right, Sheriff," Blanford confirmed. "Jocko took off right after supper. We figured he was just in town, whoopin' it up at one of the saloons. We didn't know he was plannin' to try and gun you down."

"That's the absolute truth, Sheriff," put in Denning. "When Jocko wanted to go off alone, it was dangerous to ask him where he was goin'. We sure would've done our best to talk him out of back-shootin' you if we'd known he was plannin' to do it."

Doubt was written all over Jess Packard's face. He studied the men's faces for almost a full minute, then settled his skeptical gaze on Colden. His tone threatening, he said in a dead monotone, "You'd better walk the line, Colden. One little mistake and you could end up like your friend."

The outlaws stood in silence as the lawman wheeled, walked out the doorway, and melted into the darkness. From several feet away came the sound of a saddle squeaking and hooves shuffling the soft earth, and then a tattoo of galloping hoofbeats filled the air before they quickly faded.

                    *   *   *

The next morning, Judd Colden, Vince Denning, and Mel Blanford entered Virgil Troop's office and found the mineowner talking with Curt Sibley. When Troop saw their somber faces, he grumbled, "Don't tell me . . ."

"Yeah," Colden confirmed with a nod. "Packard brought Jocko's body to the house and dumped it through the front door."

Troop swore. "So we're still saddled with the sheriff! I told Jocko that Packard wouldn't be easy to kill."

Curt Sibley's face reflected his shock. Staring at the mineowner, he asked, "Jocko Bane tried to kill the sheriff, with your approval?"

"Yeah, last night."

The youth fell silent, but it was obvious that he was nonplussed.

Colden lifted his hat, ran his fingers through his long, greasy hair, and said, "I've been thinkin' about this all night, Virgil, and there's only one sure way to kill Packard: a gun trap."

The mineowner looked puzzled. "What's that?"

"Catch him in a spot where he's real vulnerable and surround him so's he can't get away, then riddle him full of bullets." Laughing, Colden added, "It's worked for us before. Ain't that right, boys?"

Denning and Blanford affirmed that they had rid the world of several lawmen in just such a way.

Young Sibley's face paled. Turning to the mineowner, he pleaded, "Virgil, you can't let this happen! Gunning the sheriff down is going too far!"

"Shut up!" Troop ordered. "Something's gotta be done. Packard's standing in my way—and anybody who stands in my way has to die."

Sibley suddenly looked as though he had been punched in the stomach. His face as white as a sheet, he stared at the mineowner and said quietly, "Those three strangers I saw you talking with the day before Web Kirgan was murdered, they were the ones who did it, weren't they? You hired them to murder your partner so you could have the Young America all to yourself!"

Troop smiled slyly. "Yeah, kid. I hired 'em. Like I said, anybody who stands in my way . . . and Web stood in my way. I couldn't very well own the whole mine if I had a partner, now, could I?"

"You murdered your partner—a man you'd worked with for years—and now you're going to have these men murder Sheriff Packard in cold blood," Sibley said hoarsely.

"You listen to me!" Troop bellowed, grabbing Sibley by the shoulders and shaking him. "What I say goes, understand? And I don't want to hear any sass from you! Who saved your skin from those Indians? And who took you in and gave you a home? Me, that's who! I've set you up good, kid! You've already benefited aplenty from the gold and silver we've pulled out of this mine, and I've told you what it'll mean to you in the future. You owe me your life—and you owe me your loyalty! I want you to stop speaking out against what I see fit to do!"

Sibley swallowed hard. His voice was trembling as he said, "Those two Winnemucca men who were gunned down when the sheriff was out of town day before yesterday—you ordered that done, didn't you?"

"You bet. Judd and Jocko did it for me. It was necessary, to keep Art Uzelac off balance," the mineowner asserted. "You need to wake up and realize that I know what I'm doing—and keep your mouth shut. After all, these killings will eventually benefit you, too. I got a real good plan."

Cowering, the youth fell silent.

Colden asked, "What's this plan you're talkin' about, Virgil?"

"Simple," Troop replied. "Once Packard is dead, I'll move in and take over the Winnemucca mine. I've wanted this all along, but Packard's been a real obstacle. Since you've come up with a way to kill him, I can go ahead with my plan . . . and you can be sure I'll share the wealth with you and your men."

Colden looked at Blanford and Denning, grinned avariciously, then remarked, "This is gonna work out real good, 'cause I already decided that me and my boys'd take over Aurora and install our own lawmen. Linkin' up with you and your two mines will enable all of us to get filthy rich."

Clamping a hand on Colden's shoulder, Troop chuckled and stated, "You and I think a lot alike, my friend. We're gonna get along famously." He then suggested, "It's time to go about the day's work. Let's meet down at the big house shortly after sundown to make plans for this gun trap of yours. And it'd be real good if you could set it up so the three deputies are killed at the same time you wipe out Packard."

Late in the afternoon, Judd Colden, Vince Denning, and Mel Blanford returned to the big house for the evening. Dismounting, the three outlaws were approaching the rear of the house when suddenly three Paiute boys bounded from the back porch.

"Grab 'em!" Colden shouted, reaching for the one closest to him, while Denning and Blanford gave chase and seized the other two. The boys all tried to wriggle free, shouting at the top of their lungs for the white men to let them go, but the men merely laughed.

The back door opened, and George Locke and Gene Ortiz appeared. "What's goin' on, boss?" Locke asked.

Fingering the bandage on his head, he grumbled, "All that noise is givin' me a headache."

"We caught these red brats tryin' to steal somethin'," replied Colden.

The boy he was holding strained against Colden's strong hands and retorted, "We were not going to steal anything! We were just looking—"

Colden slapped the boy violently across the face, cutting off his words. "You're a dirty redskinned liar! You had no other reason for bein' on the porch!" Pulling his gun and cocking it, he said to Denning and Blanford, "Let's kill 'em!"

The men all looked stunned.

Shaking his head slowly, Locke stated, "Boss, I don't think that's a smart thing to do. I think you oughta just let 'em go."

Colden looked at him as if he were seeing him for the first time. "What are you talkin' about, George? They're filthy savages! They were gonna steal from us! I thought you hated redskins as much as I do."

"I do . . . but they're only boys," Locke argued. "They ain't more than nine or ten years old. Maybe they were just bein' curious. Anyway, what's there to steal back here?"

Colden glared at Locke. "You goin' soft? Little Indians grow up to be *big* Indians!"

Gene Ortiz shook his head. "Judd, George's right. If you kill 'em, there'll be real trouble from the tribe. It ain't worth it."

Sneering, Colden rasped, "Aw, there ain't gonna be no trouble, Gene. They won't even know what happened to these little thieves. We'll kill 'em and dump their bodies where no one'll ever find 'em."

Holding one of the boys by the arm, Mel Blanford wiped cold sweat from his face and gasped, "Judd, this

ain't right. I've never argued with you before, but
if you're suggestin' that I kill a little kid, I can't do
it."

Colden's eyes glinted, and he grinned coldly. "Why,
Mel," he said with mockery in his voice, "I wouldn't
ask you to go against your conscience." He had barely
finished speaking when he turned his gun on the boy
that Blanford held and fired at the boy's head, killing
him instantly. The other two children screamed.

While the hardened outlaws looked on, frozen with
shock, Colden first pointed his revolver at the Indian
Denning was holding and put a slug through the boy's
heart, and then he placed his weapon against the head
of the one he held and fired. Letting the boy drop, the
gang leader looked down at the body and grinned—
unaware that a fourth Paiute boy was staring in horrified disbelief from his hiding place in a nearby stand of
piñon trees.

Tearing his eyes away from the grisly sight and knowing he must get help, the frightened child reasoned that
since he was closer to Aurora than to his village, he
would run to Sheriff Jess Packard, who was a friend to
his people. Bending low, he silently threaded his way
through the trees until he was out of sight of the house,
then darted into town.

Ignoring the stares of his men, who still seemed too
stunned to react, Judd Colden casually broke open his
gun and began reloading it. A look of satisfaction was on
his face as he remarked, "See, fellas. Nothin' to it.
Three dead redskins, and who's to know I did it?"

Mel Blanford finally cleared his throat and pointed
out, "Judd, Virgil's gonna be here any minute. It might
be best if you don't let him know what you did."

"Good idea. He might not take too kindly to the
notion that I eliminated three redskin brats. How about

you boys helping me stash the bodies under the porch? We can get rid of them tomorrow."

No sooner had the bodies been hidden when Vince Denning looked over at the road and saw Troop coming down the hill from the mine. Moments later another man appeared, this one walking up from town. The second man waved and also headed toward the house, and Denning squinted to make him out in the rapidly setting sun. "Fellas," he announced, "Alex Packard's comin'."

The Paiute boy arrived in Aurora and, after getting directions from a passerby, dashed to the sheriff's office. Scared and crying, the child told Jess Packard that his name was Pamino and described what had happened at the big house. Packard was filled with wrath. Not only had Colden murdered three defenseless children, but the horrible deed might well cause the Paiutes to go on the warpath.

Telling the boy to stay at the office, Packard jammed an extra revolver under his belt and raced out to find his deputies. But all three were busy handling trouble in the saloons, so throwing caution to the wind, Packard ran out of town and headed for the big house—determined to make Judd Colden pay this time.

Twilight was falling when the enraged lawman drew near the big house. Packard was within thirty yards of the place when, through the open doorway, he heard an indistinct shout, followed by a gunshot. Suddenly bullets were chewing the ground at his feet and whizzing past his head. Pulling both revolvers, the sheriff dropped behind a piñon tree and opened fire, putting bullets through the open front door and two front windows.

His blood boiling because of Colden and his men,

Packard was not even concerned that he was greatly outnumbered. Drawing a bead on a form in the window at his right, he fired, and he smiled with satisfaction when the man howled and fell. Packard then sent a bullet through the other window, and when two shots came in return, he blasted the same window again.

More shots then came from the window, and the sheriff was about to open fire on it when a shadow appeared at the edge of the doorway. Quickly taking aim, he fired and saw the man go down. He then turned his guns back on the window to the right, put two more bullets through it, and heard a man scream.

The gun battle went on for several more minutes as the seasoned lawman emptied his guns into the house. Several times bullets flew perilously close to his head, but none of them found their mark. His hammers clicked on empty chambers, and when he had reloaded both weapons, he cautiously moved steadily closer, blasting away at the windows and the open door and filling the house with hot lead.

Suddenly the gunfire ceased. Packard leapt to his feet and zigzagged toward the house at a flat-out run, then jumped onto the porch, flattening himself against the wall near the door. All was quiet, but he knew it could be just a trick to lure him inside and pepper him with slugs. The lawman was sure he had hit at least three men, possibly more, but he had no way of knowing just how many men were inside.

The silence was abruptly broken by the sound of galloping hooves, coming from the back of the house. Dashing in that direction, Packard peered through the dusk to see two men riding away. The lawman cursed and returned to the front of the house, carefully stepping up onto the porch with both guns cocked and ready. No sound came from inside. Inching his way to the doorway, he peered inside and saw Virgil Troop lying on his back in a pool of his own blood, a slug in his midsection but still alive and conscious.

The sheriff had just entered the house and was a few feet away from Troop when the mineowner raised his head and brought up his gun. Packard fired from the hip, putting a slug through Troop's left eye.

His ears ringing from the shot fired in close quarters, the sheriff looked around through the cloud of blue smoke, ready to use his guns again, but there was no movement of any kind. He made out a lamp on a nearby table and warily stepped over to it, keeping an eye on the deeper shadows at the back of the room, then lit the lamp to dispel the gathering darkness.

The light showed Gene Ortiz lying dead at one front window, while at the other window Mel Blanford lay with a bullet through his neck. With two of Judd Colden's men dead, that left two more plus Colden himself. Only two riders had galloped away, which meant one more was somewhere . . . unless one of the gang had not been at the house when the gunfight started.

Suddenly a moan came from a dark corner at the back of the room. Holstering one gun, Packard picked up the lamp and followed a trail of blood leading from the door to the corner, figuring he had found the missing man. He reached the crumpled form and lifted the lamp higher to shed more light—and a chill slithered down his spine.

"Alex!" he choked, his throat feeling as though it were being squeezed. The younger Packard lay on his back with his hands over his abdomen. He had been gut-shot and was losing blood fast.

Stunned, Packard knelt and set the lamp on the floor. Alex was glassy-eyed but it was clear that he recognized his older brother.

"Alex!" the lawman breathed again.

Alex tried to speak, but he could merely grunt. His eyes widened for a couple of seconds, and then he emitted a final rattling breath before going limp in death.

The realization of what had happened hit Jess Packard like a bolt of lightning. In agony, he hugged his sides and began sobbing. Then he reached for his sibling, and holding Alex's body in his arms, the lawman moaned, "I killed him! I killed my own brother!"

Chapter Twelve

After quelling the trouble in the saloons, deputies Lee Austin, Ed Murdock, and Neil Thurston returned to the sheriff's office and found the young Paiute boy Pamino sitting on a chair. The child told them about the murders at the big house and that Sheriff Jess Packard had gone there alone.

Not bothering to take the time to saddle their horses, they raced on foot under a canopy of twinkling stars. They arrived at the house and approached the front porch with drawn guns, and Austin called out, "Sheriff! Are you in there?"

There was a moment of silence, then just as Austin was about to call out again, Packard replied dully, "Yes, I'm here, Lee."

The trio stepped through the door into the parlor, which was eerily quiet and barely lit by a single low-burning lamp. Nearly stumbling over three bodies, the deputies looked toward the back of the room and found Jess Packard sitting in a chair, staring down at a bloody corpse. The lifeless form was his brother.

Exchanging horrified glances, the deputies rushed to their boss's side, and Ed Murdock asked softly, "What happened, Sheriff? The Indian boy told us about his friends being killed, but . . . but what was Alex doing here? How did he get shot?"

Feeling as if his heart was as heavy as lead, Packard

slowly told his deputies that the outlaws had opened fire on him, and he returned fire, having no idea Alex was inside. His voice broke as he looked up with swollen, tear-filled eyes and choked out, "I killed him. I killed my own brother."

A weighty silence filled the room.

After a few seconds, Lee Austin queried, "Who are the other three?"

Several moments passed before Packard responded. "What? Oh. Uh . . . Troop, Ortiz, and Blanford. Two others got away on horses after the shooting stopped. I don't know who they were, since I haven't been able to find the other gang member."

Lee Austin found another lamp and lit it, then left the others, saying he was going to take a look out back. Within minutes the deputy returned, and setting the lamp on a small table in a corner, he said, "It seems the two who took off on the horses were Colden and Denning, 'cause George Locke is sprawled on the back steps, deader than a doornail. You hit him in the chest, Sheriff. Looks like he had intentions of getting away, too, but he never made it."

Packard idly nodded. "Thanks, Lee. Now I know who I have to track down."

After a brief stretch of silence, Neil Thurston looked down at the seated Packard and remarked, "Sheriff, I hate to say this, but it's got to be brought up. It sure seems like Alex had something going with these outlaws. He certainly was spending a lot of time with them, especially at the saloons . . . and everybody in town knows that he suddenly had a lot of money to spend."

Packard merely stared at his brother's lifeless face, as if he would find some answers there.

Ed Murdock cleared his throat and put in, "I have to agree with Neil. Finding Alex here tonight with these characters leaves little doubt that he was linked up with them. And it sure was strange that your brother asked you to go hunting with him—and just coincidentally, while you and Alex were out of town, those two Winnemucca men were murdered."

Sickened to the point of nausea, Jess Packard scrubbed a shaky hand over his face and raised his head. Without looking at any one man in particular, he admitted in a gravelly voice, "I've had the same thoughts running through my head ever since I found Alex here. But somehow I can't accept what seems to be obvious. I knew my brother, and Alex would not join with criminals. All his life he's been as honest and straightforward as a person can be and loyal to a fault. That's why he wouldn't give up on Vince Denning. My brother had a big heart, and it was a faithful heart, besides. He loved his wife and children, and I just can't believe he'd mix himself up in something that might hurt them. I know what it looks like, but I'm telling you, my brother was not in on something shady with these outlaws."

Austin squeezed the sheriff's shoulder and murmured, "I sure hope you're right, Sheriff. I sure do. And if there's a way to clear Alex's name, I hope it can be found."

Packard's eyes filled with tears, and his voice broke as he said, "My greater burden is that I . . . I killed my own brother."

Sympathizing, the deputies offered to carry Alex's body back to town.

Packard nodded, then pointed out, "We need to find the bodies of those Paiute boys and their horses. I'll have to take them to the village tomorrow."

"We can come back in the morning and do that, Sheriff," Austin suggested. "We wouldn't be able to search in the dark, anyway." He then added, "I'll take Pamino home with me for the night and bring him to the office first thing in the morning. He's too young to be riding alone back to his village."

Sighing, a disheartened Jess Packard followed the deputies as they bore Alex's corpse to the undertaking parlor. When that sad task had been completed, the lawman told his men, "I've got to go and break the awful news to Lola."

"I'll go with you, Sheriff," offered Murdock.

Shaking his head, Packard replied, "It's better that I do it alone, Ed. I appreciate your offer, but this is a family matter."

The heavyhearted sheriff headed for the Packard house, and the dread of telling his sister-in-law that Alex had died from a bullet inflicted by his own brother made Packard feel sick all over. Reaching the small, low-roofed house, he trudged up the porch steps, and his hands trembled as he knocked on the door. The door came open to reveal Lola clad in a robe and slippers, her long, dark hair hanging loosely on her shoulders.

"Hello, Jess," she said, stepping back to allow him to enter. Shaking her head in consternation, she continued, "If you're looking for your brother, he's not here. I assume he's at one of the saloons, playing poker with Vince Denning." Then Lola cocked her head, closely studying the lawman's face. "Jess, what's wrong? You look as though you've been crying."

"Something dreadful has happened, Lola," Packard replied, his voice quavering.

The brunette's hand went to her mouth. "What? Is it Alex? Has he been hurt?"

Closing the door behind him, the lawman choked, "Maybe . . . maybe you should sit down."

Lola's face paled, and she stepped close to Packard, staring intently into his eyes. "Just tell me, Jess! Tell me what's happened to Alex!"

Packard took hold of her shoulders, guided her to a

chair, and sat her down. Glancing around, he asked softly, "Are the children in bed?"

"Yes," she replied, adding urgently, "Please! Tell me what has happened to Alex!"

Dropping to one knee and looking directly into her eyes, the lawman swallowed with difficulty and said falteringly, "Alex . . . Alex is dead, Lola."

Lola Packard gasped and threw her hands to her face. Her eyes huge with disbelief, she finally managed to whisper, "H-how did it h-happen?"

Packard felt as though his heart was going to turn to stone as he told her, "A bullet—a bullet that came from *my* gun. It . . . it was totally unintentional, but . . . but I killed Alex."

Lola stared at her brother-in-law incredulously, and her body began to quake. "I . . . I don't understand," she breathed.

The lawman slowly and methodically told Lola about the Paiute boys being murdered by Judd Colden and how he had gone to the house to arrest the outlaw and ended up in a gun battle. He broke down and wept several times as he recounted finding Alex near death with a bullet in his stomach.

When Packard had finished, Lola began whimpering like a wounded kitten. The sheriff took her into his arms, and she clung to him as if trying to draw strength from him. Finally the whimpering turned to tormented sobbing, and her body shook violently. Packard held her tight, shedding tears of his own, and let her cry it out.

When she had regained a degree of composure, she drew back and looked into her brother-in-law's dark brown eyes and whispered, "Oh, Jess, how utterly horrible for you! I know how much you loved Alex. It must be almost more than you can bear!"

"I'll never get over it," he responded, gritting his teeth. "Never."

Shaking her head slowly, Lola stroked his face tenderly and told him, "But you can't blame yourself, Jess. You had no way of knowing Alex was in the house. He . . . he shouldn't have been there. As much as it hurts me to say it—especially now—everything seems to point to Alex's having linked himself with Colden and his men."

Bowing his head, Packard softly responded, "I know it appears that way, Lola, but I still can't believe Alex was guilty of that. It wasn't in him to be involved in anything outside the law. Somehow I've got to clear his name—and the only way I know to do it is to track down Colden and Denning and make them tell me what was going on and why Alex was at the house tonight. Besides, Colden has to be brought in for murdering those Indian boys."

After riding hard until it became too dark to see, Judd Colden and Vince Denning hauled up in a ravine at the base of Sonora Pass. Dismounting and walking his sweat-soaked horse around, Colden remarked, "There ain't gonna be a moon tonight, Vince, so it's too dangerous to keep ridin'. We'll have to hole up right here till dawn."

"That could be dangerous, too," Denning objected. "Packard's gonna be on our tails with a posse as sure as anything. We need to get to San Andreas and join up with Bob Reedy and the rest of the boys as soon as possible. I don't think Packard's gonna let it bother him that we're in California. You can bet your boots he'll chase us as far as he has to in order to get us. We'll have a chance if we can get to San Andreas."

"I agree with you, my friend," Colden responded, "but one or both of us slippin' over the edge of a cliff ain't gonna do us no good. 'Sides, if it's too dark for us to ride, it's too dark for a posse to ride. We'll head out at first light."

Pulling his jacket tighter and fending off the cool of the evening, the gang leader added, "And since we've got us a good head start, we're gonna take a few minutes to stop at the way station at the top of the pass and take care of the McGuires. They've got it comin'."

Sheriff Jess Packard and his deputies had been in the office only a few minutes at the beginning of the new day when Ed Murdock looked out the window and reported, "Sheriff, there's a big crowd gathering out there—and it doesn't look any too friendly."

Before Packard could comment, a loud voice from outside demanded, "Sheriff Packard, we want to talk to you!"

The lawman recognized Gus Widner's voice and muttered, "No doubt the Aurora grapevine has spread the news of Alex's death to the last dog and cat, and I'm sure I know what the commotion's about." With that, he opened the door and stepped out on the boardwalk, and the deputies walked out behind him.

Widner was standing at the forefront of the crowd, flanked by other leaders of the town, including Derek Wood, who was chairman of the town council. The saloon owner said, "Jess, I know it must've come mighty hard when you finished the shoot-out last night and found that you'd killed Alex—but let's face it, it wouldn't have happened if he hadn't been there. The other day you convinced a lot of us that your brother wasn't linked up with the Colden gang in any way . . . but if that's the case, how do you explain his being there with them when the shooting started last night?"

Before Packard could speak, Art Uzelac stepped beside Widner and asked loudly, "You knew your brother was in cahoots with the Colden gang, didn't you? A man would have to be blind to miss the fact that Alex had money hanging out of his pockets—which he didn't have until those outlaws rode into town!"

"That's right, Jess!" Derek Wood concurred. "Looks to me like your brother was getting dirty money from Colden. You couldn't help but know about it, but you covered for him. How come? Was it because you were getting some cash under the table yourself?"

Packard was about to snap back at Wood when he saw Monica threading her way through the crowd, heading for her father. Suddenly another man bellowed, "Looks to me like our upstanding sheriff was plannin' to worm his way into the Young America mine, but somethin' went wrong, and that was the real reason for the gunfight! He probably started blazin' away at the big house last night not realizin' that his brother was inside!"

"Yeah, it's obvious the sheriff was in cahoots with Troop and his scoundrels!" shouted a woman from the middle of the crowd. "Why else would he have been out of town the day the Winnemucca men were murdered?"

"That's right!" Art Uzelac shouted above the loud rumble of the crowd. "Who were you planning to allow the Colden bunch to murder next, Packard? Me? You and Troop were probably gonna eliminate me and try to take over the Winnemucca next! What went wrong? Did Troop decide to squeeze you out and keep it all for himself?"

The crowd was fast turning into a mob. Raising his hands, the sheriff called for the people to calm down so he could speak in his own defense, but no sooner had the hubbub subsided somewhat than a man at the back of the crowd shouted, "Seems to me you oughta resign, Packard! You've dirtied your badge!"

One by one, voices shouted for Jess Packard's resignation, and soon the crowd was again at a fever pitch. A red-faced Derek Wood shook a fist at Packard and screamed, "That's right, Packard! Take off that badge! There's mud on it!"

The publisher's words fired up the citizens all the more.

Lee Austin looked at the other deputies and muttered, "I've had enough of this." Whipping out his gun, he fired it twice into the air.

The sharp reports had an immediate effect on the crowd. As the people quieted down, an angry Austin looked over the sea of faces and declared, "You're all acting like a pack of wild dogs! Let the sheriff have his say!"

A silence fell over the crowd as all eyes riveted on Packard, who was struggling with his temper. He had spent a sleepless night, his remorse over killing his brother eating away at him, and the accusations of Aurora's townspeople were almost more than he could bear. Agitation was written all over him as he declared, "None of what you people are saying makes sense. I came to Esmeralda County and pinned on this badge because you asked me to, and not once in all these years have you had any cause for complaint. If you suddenly feel I'm not doing a good job of keeping law and order here, then fire me—but don't throw unfounded and unproven charges at me."

"I've seen proof enough!" Wood shouted. "You and your no-good brother had a moneymaking scheme going with those outlaws. You got caught, so now you're arching your back. Why don't you just have enough decency to resign and get out of our town?" Turning to his daughter, who stood beside him, the publisher asked, "Aren't those your sentiments, Monica? Tell the truth now. Don't be afraid of Jess. None of us will let him hurt you."

Monica's face colored, and as she looked around at her neighbors, all of whom were denouncing Jess Packard and encouraging her to do likewise, it was readily apparent that the lawman had lost his constituency's admiration and support and was through in Esmeralda County. Briefly looking at her father, who nodded and smiled, she turned toward Packard and said coldly, "I completely agree with my father and everyone else. I've also had my suspicions about Alex—and I've had some of the same reservations about you as have all of these good folks. It's my feeling, too, that you didn't do anything about your brother's involvement with the Colden gang because you were reaping financial benefit yourself."

"You tell him, Miss Wood!" shouted a woman.

The encouragement seemed to strengthen Monica's resolve. Looking Packard straight in the eye, she announced, "I can no longer care for you, now that you've so badly tarnished your badge." With that, she pulled the engagement ring off her finger, walked over to the lawman, and handed it to him.

Packard stared at the ring glittering in his palm, almost doubting the reality of what was happening. At the very time he needed his woman to comfort him over the tragedy of his killing his own brother and to stand beside him while facing his accusers, she had become one of them. His heart felt like a lump of lead in his chest.

As disgust welled up in him, the lawman's face tightened with anger. Teeth clenched, he stared unwaveringly at Monica and dropped the ring at his feet, then ground it into the dirt with the heel of his boot.

Monica's eyes widened, and she wheeled and rushed to her father's open arms.

While the throng stared in silence, Packard removed his badge and looked steadily at his three deputies, all of whom had turned pale and were watching him closely. His face grim, the lawman then handed the badge to Derek Wood and told him in a voice loud enough for all to hear, "All of your accusations are unfounded. I'm going after Colden and Denning, and when I bring them back here, I'll make them tell the truth—and that'll clear my name as well as Alex's. My brother may have been guilty of poor judgment by remaining a friend of Denning's, but he was *not* guilty of any criminal activity."

As Packard started to turn away, Lee Austin spoke up, "Jess, if you're quitting, we'll quit, too. What's happened here isn't right."

Putting his hand on the deputy's shoulder, Packard told him softly, "Don't. These people still need protection. When I clear myself, maybe they'll be decent enough to apologize and ask me to wear the badge again."

Without another word, he walked into the office and got Pamino—who had been brought there by Lee Austin—and then went to get his horse. Saddling up, he took the boy and they rode to the big house, where it did not take him long to find the bodies of the three murdered boys. He covered the bodies with sheets taken from the outlaws' beds, sparing Pamino the horror of seeing his dead friends while Pamino brought the boys' ponies from their hiding place. Packard draped the bodies over three of the ponies, and Pamino rode his own. As he rode to the Paiute village, he prayed he could convince Joaquin Jim to keep the Paiutes from going on the warpath.

Arriving at the village, Packard was instantly surrounded by shocked and enraged Paiutes, who had sent out a search party that had not yet returned. Releasing

Pamino to his parents, the lawman dismounted and, after asking to see Joaquin Jim, learned that the chieftain was on a journey to northern Nevada but was expected to return at any time.

Furious voices called for revenge against the whites, but Packard pleaded with the people to understand that the murders were committed by one man, an outlaw he was pursuing. "Please, I beg you not to attack other whites for what Judd Colden did. I promise that justice will be done and Colden will be punished! I will hunt down the man who killed your boys, and he will hang!"

One of the fathers of the murdered boys shouted, "No! We do not need you to find Colden and bring justice to him! My son has been wantonly killed, and for that the truce should be broken! We should put on war paint now!"

The man's fellow villagers shouted their agreement. When Packard tried to argue, several of them swarmed the ex-lawman, throwing him to the ground. But one of the older braves, a subchief, went to Packard's aid, demanding that the people back off as he helped Packard to his feet.

"Jess Packard has proven to be a friend to our people," the old Indian loudly stated. "Do not harm him in your anger. Leave the pursuit of the white man to him. I am certain that Joaquin Jim would want it so. When our chief returns, we will tell him about the murders. If he decides to put on war paint at that time, we will do so. It is his decision to make, not ours."

The villagers fell silent.

Thanking the elderly brave, Packard promised, "You won't regret this. I swear to you that Judd Colden will pay with his life."

The stalwart subchief folded his arms and replied, "We will do nothing until Joaquin Jim arrives. What he will decide, I cannot say."

Feeling hopeful that the chieftain would be on his side, Packard mounted up and headed back to Aurora. He had two important stops to make—the first at the Young America mine to see if any of the miners had any idea where Judd Colden might have gone, and the second to see Lola.

Reaching the mine, he talked with several of the many miners who were just milling around, unclear as to what the future of the mine would be now that Virgil Troop was dead. Pressing the issue of Judd Colden and his murder of the three Paiute boys, Packard told them of the bloodshed that would come at the hands of the Indians unless Colden was caught and hanged. It took but minutes to learn that Colden had spoken of a cabin a few miles on the other side of Sonora Pass, in California. Thanking the men for their help, the ex-sheriff headed into Aurora.

Packard rode through the residential section to Lola's house. The young widow's eyes were swollen from crying, and her children's expressions were ones of incomprehension, not fully understanding why their daddy was not coming home. Fighting back his own sorrow as well as his guilt, Packard explained that he had resigned and was going after the outlaws on his own.

"Since I don't know how long it'll take to find and capture Denning and Colden," the ex-sheriff told his sister-in-law, "you should go ahead and have Alex buried." Holding Lola tight for a moment, Packard whispered, "Keep faith in Alex. Deep inside me I know he was innocent, even though the circumstances say otherwise. And I'm going to prove it if it's the last thing I do."

Nodding wordlessly, Lola's eyes filled with tears.

Packard mounted up and rode to the sheriff's office. Lee Austin was seated at Packard's old desk, and he looked slightly embarrassed when his former boss walked through the door. Packard told Austin what he had learned from the miners. "Seeing as how Colden's hideout is in California, if I had kept my badge, I wouldn't have had the authority to go after him, anyway. So it's just as well this way."

The ex-lawman took his leave of the new acting sheriff, and as Packard headed west out of town, he saw Monica walking his way. Giving her a cold look, he put his horse to a gallop, anxious to leave Aurora, and soon he was climbing into the High Sierras.

Chapter Thirteen

The sun rose into a clear sky over the Sierra Nevada range, promising a warm day even at the higher elevations, and travelers who had spent the night at the McGuire Way Station atop Sonora Pass were eating breakfast, preparing to move on. The stagecoach crew was outside, harnessing the team, when Charlie Tigman, who lived a few miles down the eastern slope of the pass, drove up in his old wagon.

"Howdy, fellas," the elderly Tigman said as he hauled the buckboard to a rattling halt.

" 'Mornin'," the crew said in unison.

Alighting from the wagon, Tigman entered the station and greeted Mamie McGuire, then asked, "How's Ev doin'?"

"A little better each day," Mamie responded, finishing pouring coffee for her customers. "He'll be up and sitting around in here a bit later. How's Flossie?"

"Well, that's what I'm here about, Mamie," he replied. "The missus is laid up with a bad leg. It's swollen somethin' awful. I've got her lyin' down with it elevated, but she's sorta helpless in that position, and the problem is, I've got to make a trip down the mountain today that'll take about three hours in all. I was wonderin' if you or Angie could stay with Flossie while I'm gone."

At that moment, the auburn-haired Angie emerged from the kitchen with an empty tray for picking up

dishes. She gave the old gentleman a warm smile and
said, "Good morning, Charlie. Did I hear you mention
my name?"

Her aunt quickly explained about Flossie Tigman,
and the two women agreed that since the morning rush
was about over and Angie was through waiting on tables, she could go and stay with their ailing neighbor.
Minutes later, Angie rode away in the buckboard with
Charlie.

It was nearing nine o'clock when Judd Colden and
Vince Denning drew near the way station and halted in
the dense timber on the south side, studying the place.
No horses were tied at the hitch rail in front, and no
vehicles were parked around.

Colden grinned maliciously and stated, "Looks right
perfect. No customers at the moment. I can't wait to fix
those people for what they did to us."

The outlaws were about to spur their mounts when
Vince Denning cautioned, "Wait a minute."

Colden followed Denning's line of sight and saw four
riders topping the crest of the pass. The gang leader
cursed them for showing up at just that time, saying
they would no doubt stop at the station, when Denning
squinted at the approaching riders and declared, "Hold
your fussin', Judd. That's Bob and the boys."

Colden gasped, "Well, I'll be a— What're they doin'
here?"

"Let's ask 'em," Denning said wryly, nudging his
horse out of the protective timber.

Following, Colden waved his hat to get the attention
of the newcomers, and Reedy and his cronies spotted
them and galloped down the slope. When they drew
up, Colden led them into the trees, asking why they
had left San Andreas and where they were going.

Bob Reedy quickly explained that San Andreas's new
marshal had once arrested Lloyd Hice and him for

robbing a stagecoach near Sacramento, and that meant
trouble would follow if they had stayed. The men had
decided to move on over the mountains and find a place
to stay in Bridgeport, and from there they could surrep-
titiously contact Colden to let him know that when
he took over Aurora, they were close by and could be
there quickly.

Reedy then asked what Colden and Denning were
doing atop the pass, and the gang leader explained the
setup that had been forming to make them all rich—
and how it had all fallen apart. Telling the new arrivals
about killing the Indian boys and the subsequent shoot-
out with Sheriff Jess Packard, Colden admitted, "Vince
and me lit out so fast, we don't even know if any of the
boys or Virgil Troop are alive. We figure Packard'll be
on our tails with a posse, and we planned to meet up
with you guys at San Andreas so's we'd have some
manpower to fight them off." Pausing, he grinned evilly,
adding, "But seein' you right here has popped an idea
into my head. If Packard was dead, we could go back to
Aurora and take up where Vince and I left off. We can
still be filthy rich."

"How we gonna kill off Packard, boss?" Franklin
Kreeger queried.

"The same way I took care of Marshal Ted Wiley and
his deputy: a gun trap. The way I figure it, even if the
posse's large, we'll have the element of surprise. What
do you boys say?"

The men were all in agreement.

Calculating that they would have about a two-hour
lead on the posse, Colden informed Reedy and his men
that he and Denning had some business to tend to at
the way station. He gave the foursome directions to the
cabin north of the pass, telling Reedy to hole up there
and wait until he and Denning arrived. The posse would
no doubt track the two of them to the cabin, which

would work out real well, for there was an ideal place close by the hideout to set up the trap.

As soon as the others had taken off, Colden and Denning rode to the way station and dismounted. Adjusting their gun belts, they entered the station and found Mamie sweeping the floor and Everett sitting in a horsehair-stuffed chair near the huge fireplace. The McGuires looked over to see who their customers were and fear showed instantly on their faces.

Holding the broom protectively as she moved close to her husband's chair, Mamie asked with a tremor in her voice, "What do you want?"

Colden glanced toward the kitchen and in an icy voice demanded, "Where's the redhead?"

"She's not here," Everett answered.

"Where is she?" the killer snapped.

"She's . . . she's gone down the mountain for the day."

His voice menacing, Colden growled, "You better not be lyin' to me."

"I'm not lying," McGuire insisted. "Search the place if you want to."

Colden swore, wanting to exact vengeance on Angie, also, but then he decided he would be satisfied to take his fury out on the couple.

"What do you want?" Mamie repeated fearfully.

The gang leader gritted his teeth and snarled, "The pleasure of payin' you people back for what you did!" Stepping closer to Everett, he looked down at him and railed, "You jumped my friend Jocko Bane when all he was doin' was havin' a little fun with your niece. That ain't very nice, McGuire."

Colden raised his hand to strike Everett when Vince Denning warned, "Hold it, Judd! There's a wagon pullin' up outside!"

Turning to look out the window, the gang leader saw three men climbing down from the wagon that had just halted by the porch. Colden eyed the McGuires and in a low, threatening voice told them, "You two better not try to get help from these guys. If you do, they'll die . . . and so will you!"

Heavy footsteps sounded on the porch, and then three trappers, armed only with knives, entered. Mamie crossed the room, asking what she could do for them, and they replied that they needed some supplies.

While Mamie waited on them at the counter, the outlaws sat close to Everett as if they were old friends and carried on a light conversation. Colden kept a close eye on Mamie to make sure she did not go into the kitchen to grab a shotgun as she had done the last time.

It took nearly twenty minutes for the trappers to make their purchases. When they were about ready to go, Colden breathed with relief—but the relief was short-lived. As they were walking to the door, the trappers abruptly lingered, deciding to chat with the outlaws and Everett McGuire. The tension in the station was almost palpable as the men talked on about their lives as trappers. Another half hour passed before they finally left.

"About time," Colden muttered, fingering the butt of his revolver as the trappers rolled away in their wagon.

Then suddenly two riders hauled up out front and dismounted. The gang leader cursed, knowing he and Denning dared not wait at the station too long if they wanted to avoid Sheriff Jess Packard and his posse—no doubt on their trail and riding hard.

Looking over at Colden, Mamie read the warning in the gang leader's eyes not to try anything. Then the door creaked open, and two muscular men entered, both wearing tied-down guns and looking tough. As

Mamie scurried over to wait on them, she told herself these newcomers could probably handle the outlaws. Somehow she must let the two men know about the situation, for she was certain that she and Everett would be killed by Colden, regardless.

"Good morning, gentlemen," she said, trying her best to mask her fear. "What can I do for you?"

The shorter of the two men replied, "We just need some tobacco, ma'am."

Mamie led them to the counter where various tins of tobacco and other items were lined up on a shelf. While they deliberated over their selection, the frightened woman stood behind the counter and cast a fleeting glance at Colden and Denning. They were watching her intently. But Mamie was determined to get help, and with cold sweat beading her brow, she kept her trembling hands low and out of their sight while scribbling on a slip of paper with a pencil stub. The letters were shaky but legible and spelled out but two words: *Outlaws! Help!*

The travelers finally laid their choices on the countertop, and the taller man asked, "What's the total, ma'am?"

"Well, let's see, here," Mamie mumbled, trying to add up the prices of the assorted items mentally. But her mind was so numb with fear, she was unable to make the calculation. "That'll be a dollar seventy-five," she finally estimated.

"I think you're a little off, there, ma'am," the man said evenly.

"Oh, of course," Mamie replied nervously. "How could I have made such a mistake? Believe me, I wouldn't overcharge you on purpose."

"You weren't overcharging us, ma'am," the tough-looking man stated, showing a hint of a smile. "I think you were cheating yourself out of fifty cents."

Shaking her head, Mamie responded lightly, "So I was. I must be getting old. I sure never used to have this problem."

The shorter man peered at her trembling hands and asked, "Are you all right, ma'am?"

From the corner of her eye, Mamie saw Colden and Denning tense up. "Oh, ah . . . yes. I'm fine. Just not feeling my best today, thank you."

The taller man gave Mamie the correct amount. Placing the money in the cash drawer, she murmured, "I'll put these things in a sack for you."

Mamie slipped the folded note between her fingers and dropped the tobacco tins and cigarette papers inside a small paper sack. When she handed the man the sack, she pressed the note against his palm, saying, "There you are, sir. Thanks for being so honest."

The look in his eyes told her he understood what was going on and would read the note immediately. As the riders stepped outside, Mamie nervously wiped the moisture from her brow.

Having figured out what she did, Colden growled angrily to Denning, "She slipped those guys a note! I'm sure of it!" Then he glared at McGuire and warned, "If you so much as move or say a word, you and your wife both die this minute!"

With a jerk of his head, the gang leader indicated the door and whipped out his gun. "Come on, Vince. Those two will be comin' back inside any second!"

Mamie stood at the counter and stared in horror as the outlaws headed toward the front door, guns cocked and ready. His eyes blazing, Colden glared at Mamie and muttered, "You've done it now, lady. And if you open your mouth to warn 'em, I'll put a bullet through your husband's head!"

The terrified woman stood rooted to the spot. She

cast a fearful look at her husband, who remained in his chair, also unmoving.

Motioning for Denning to stand against the wall so he would be hidden when the door came open, Colden then flattened himself against the wall on the other side of the door. The inside of the way station was completely hushed as everyone listened for sounds of the two men returning.

A half minute had passed when soft footfalls were heard just outside the door. Suddenly the door flew open, covering Vince Denning. The taller man entered first, his gun drawn and cocked, while his shorter companion was right behind him. Both men halted just inside the room and looked all around.

Suddenly Judd Colden raised his revolver, pointed it at the shorter man's head, and asked dryly, "Lookin' for somebody?"

The travelers immediately pivoted, their pistols aimed, but Colden pulled the trigger, sending a bullet through the shorter man's brain, while at the same time, Denning kicked the door closed and blasted the taller one in the heart. Mamie screamed as the sharp reports echoed and clattered inside the room, and both men collapsed, dead.

Climbing over the bodies to get to Mamie, a furious Colden swore at her for her stupidity and hit her violently with his fist. She went down hard, slamming against the floor and badly bruising her cheek.

While Mamie lay stunned, Colden swore again as he glared at her husband, who was on his feet and heading as fast as he could move for the kitchen, where the shotguns were kept. But the gang leader ran across the room and intercepted McGuire, cracking the station owner across the temple with the gun butt.

When McGuire fell, the vicious outlaw savagely

and repeatedly kicked him in the face, bloodying him badly.

While Colden loomed over McGuire, who lay on the floor, shaking his head to clear it, Vince Denning stood over Mamie, grinning maliciously. "Now we can have some fun, right, Judd?"

"You got that right, Vince," Colden replied smugly. "Follow me."

The couple were picked up by the outlaws and laid facedown and side by side on one of the large tables in the eating area. Using hemp cords found in the storeroom, Colden and Denning bound Mamie's and McGuire's ankles and wrists to the legs of the table. When the pair were secure, Colden stood over them and crowed, "Well, McGuire, this is what you get for jumpin' my friend Jocko. And you, lady, you're about to get your reward for puttin' a shotgun on us. I just wish that pretty little niece of yours was here to get hers. Guess we'll just have to take care of her some other time."

"What are you going to do?" the station owner asked, his voice quavering.

"You'll see, my friend. You'll see." Turning to Denning, Colden instructed, "Vince, I saw a five-gallon can of kerosene in the storeroom when we were getting the rope. Go get it."

While Denning headed for the storeroom, Mamie, shaking with terror, looked up at Colden and moaned, "You . . . you're not going to burn us!"

Colden grinned wickedly, and his eyes burned with malice. "Oh, yes, we are."

"Colden!" McGuire shouted. "You can't do this! Please! Have mercy!"

Ignoring the man's plea, Colden demanded, "Where'd you put the guns you stole from us?"

Mamie asked in a thin voice, "If I tell you, will you not do this awful thing?"

Reaching down and grabbing a handful of her hair, Colden jerked her head back hard and warned through gritted teeth, "Tell me, or I'll break your neck!"

"Th-they're under the counter," she gasped.

Denning returned with the kerosene. Colden took the can from him and said, "Our guns are under the counter. Get 'em."

The couple watched with terror-filled eyes as Judd Colden poured kerosene on the floor in a wide circle around the table where they were tied. He then splashed it on tables and chairs outside the ring, and when the can was empty and the room was filled with the rank odor of kerosene, Colden let it clatter to the floor and pulled a match from his shirt pocket.

Striding outside the ring of kerosene, the vicious outlaw eyed the McGuires and gleefully chuckled. "Thought I'd put you in a circle of fire so's you could watch it close you in real slow-like." Striking the match, he announced, "Nobody puts a shotgun on Judd Colden and gets away with it."

The outlaw dropped the match into the flammable liquid and the kerosene immediately burst into flame and began to work its way around the circle. Colden then dropped two more lit matches where he had spilled the fuel on the tables and chairs, laughed heartily, and led his partner outside. Listening to the crackling of the fire, the outlaws mounted up and galloped away.

Angie McGuire and Charlie Tigman were driving in a leisurely way up the pass toward the crest, talking about Flossie's illness, when suddenly Angie spotted pillars of black smoke curling into the sky.

"Charlie!" she exclaimed, pointing. "Look!"

The old man gasped, "That has to be the way station, honey!"

"Hurry!" she demanded, grabbing his arm.

Tigman snapped the reins and shouted at the team, and the horses pressed into the harness and galloped as fast as they could up the steep incline. Biting her lower lip, Angie hoped her aunt and uncle were all right.

When the bounding wagon reached the top of the crest, Angie gasped at the sight. The station building was swathed in flames, and thick smoke was billowing out the windows and through the open door. Above the roaring fire, Mamie's screams could be discerned.

"Charlie!" Angie cried. "They must be trapped inside!"

She stared in horror at the black smoke wreathing the doorway, and beyond the smoke she could see sheets of flame licking at the walls. Angie started toward the door, but the old man caught her by the arm, warning, "You can't go in there! You'll burn to death!"

Pulling loose from his grasp, the redhead argued, "I have to try! I can't just let them die!"

Suddenly Angie was aware of pounding hoofbeats coming up behind them. Whirling about, she was surprised to see Jess Packard galloping up. The horse was still in motion as the tall man leapt out of the saddle several yards from where she stood. Angie ran to him, crying, "Jess! My aunt and uncle are trapped inside the building! Charlie and I just got here and found the place in flames!"

Packard looked quickly around. "Is there anything I can use to wrap myself in? A saddle blanket or something?"

The elderly neighbor pointed to his buckboard. "I've got a blanket in back."

Grabbing the blanket, Packard removed his hat and handed it to Angie, telling her, "I'll get them out. Don't worry."

He immediately ran to the trough that stood near the hitch rail, plunged the blanket into the water, and draped the sodden material over his head and shoulders. Without pausing, he bolted through the doorway into the blazing building. Mamie's screams were still audible above the roar of the flames, and Angie stood wide-eyed, holding her breath, as Packard disappeared in the cloud of smoke.

With the room obscured by the thick smoke, Packard's feet tangled with a body sprawled just inside the doorway, and he fell down in a heap. He quickly got to his feet, then blinked against the smoke and examined the men's bodies, fearing that one of them was Everett McGuire. But they were strangers to him, and both had been shot. Wheeling about, he followed the sound of Mamie's screams and halted at the edge of the circle of the flames. Through the crackling fire, he could see the McGuires tied facedown on the table. The flames were about eight feet from them.

Using the wet blanket as a shield, he dashed through the flames to the table and shouted, "Hang on, folks! I'll get you out!"

He pulled out his pocketknife and cut the cords, freeing the couple, and then he yelled above the roar, "I'll take your wife out first, Mr. McGuire! Then I'll be back for you!"

Coughing violently, McGuire nodded as Packard wrapped the blanket around Mamie and used what was left to help cover his face. "All right, ma'am, here we go!"

Packard safely escorted Mamie out of the blazing building, then soaked the blanket again and went back in for her husband. When the second rescue had been successfully completed, the ex-lawman stood gasping for fresh air while Everett and Mamie McGuire, tears streaming down their faces, stood beside their neighbor's wagon and watched their way station going up in smoke.

Certain that he knew the answer even before posing

the question, Packard asked what had happened. McGuire, whose face was caked with blood, told him that Judd Colden and Vince Denning had come seeking revenge. Packard was furious and even more determined than ever to catch the murderous outlaws.

Assessing the fire, Packard asked if the horses should be gotten out of the barn, but the McGuires assured him that the barn was far enough away from the station building that it would be in no danger of catching fire.

"I have a question of my own," Angie put in, staring at Packard. "What are you doing here?"

Sighing, he explained about the shoot-out at the big house and of Alex's death from a bullet that he had fired. "The whole town turned against me and accused me of being in cahoots with Troop and Colden, demanding my resignation," he went on. "So I turned in my badge and went looking for Colden and Denning. The only way I'll clear my name and Alex's is by capturing them and bringing them in."

Suddenly Angie's arms were around the ex-lawman, and she murmured sympathetically, "Oh, Sheriff, it's no wonder there's such bitterness in your voice and so much hurt in your eyes. My heart just breaks for you."

The closeness and warmth of the beautiful young woman stirred Packard, and he found his arms automatically closing around her slim body. When she released him and stepped back slightly, he gave her a sad smile and told her quietly, "Thank you, Angie. You're a loyal friend." Then the smile disappeared and his voice turned steely. "That's a lot more than I can say for my former fiancée. Monica turned on me like everyone else in Aurora and publicly broke our engagement."

The redhead's eyes widened in surprise momentarily, but then she said, "I . . . I'm sorry things turned out badly with Monica."

Shaking his head slowly, Packard responded, "Don't

be. Our marriage probably wouldn't have worked out, anyway. Monica obviously didn't really love me, or she would have believed in me and stood by me. I can see now what she loved was the badge I wore and the prestige that went with it. She killed any feelings I had for her. All I feel now is relief that she showed her true colors *before* the wedding took place."

Angie was silent for a long moment, then noted, "I guess I can't call you Sheriff anymore. May I call you Jess?"

"You already did," he replied with a grin. "When I first rode up."

"Oh," she said, blushing. "I didn't mean—"

"It's all right. Besides, I just called you Angie."

Cocking her head, she looked at him intently, a soft smile on her lips, and again Packard felt a stirring within. "So you did," she said softly.

Charlie Tigman spoke up and invited the McGuires to stay at his home until the way station could be rebuilt, and they quickly accepted. As the McGuires piled into the buckboard, Packard asked if they knew of a cabin in the vicinity that was unoccupied. Everett McGuire described one a few miles to the north that hunters and trappers often stayed in, and when the ex-lawman relayed what the miners had told him, the station owner commented that it was probably the very cabin where Colden and Denning were holed up.

Angie suddenly laid a hand on Packard's arm and said, "I don't think you should go there alone. Can't you find someone to go with you?"

"There's no time to gather forces, Angie," he replied, drinking in her beauty and suddenly wishing he did not have to leave. "I've got to catch those scum as soon as possible. But if you'll tell me how to find Mr. Tigman's place, I'll stop by on the way back . . . with the outlaws in tow."

Angie gave him directions, pointing eastward down the pass. Nodding, Packard turned toward his horse and was about to mount up when the redhead gripped his sleeve and pulled him around. Standing on her tiptoes, she planted a kiss on his cheek and said urgently, "Please be careful, Jess!"

Touching the spot with his fingertips as if it were suddenly sacred, Jess Packard smiled and replied, "I'll be careful . . . and I look forward to seeing you real soon."

Chapter Fourteen

Judd Colden and Vince Denning arrived at the cabin and found the rest of the gang lounging around on the porch, smoking cigarettes and drinking whiskey. Leaping down off their horses, they hurried over to the foursome.

Rising to meet them, Bob Reedy flipped a half-smoked cigarette onto the bare earth surrounding the cabin and said, "You look like you're expectin' Packard real soon, boss."

"I am," Colden confirmed, nodding. "Our business at the way station took longer than I figured, and that stinkin' sheriff could be showin' up with his posse at any time now. Let's go inside."

When the gang had gathered around the cabin's crude table, Colden looked at Wes Ardahl and asked, "You still carry them field glasses in your saddlebag?"

"Sure do," Ardahl answered, blowing smoke toward the ceiling.

"Okay. Get 'em."

When Ardahl returned, the gang leader instructed, "Sit over there by the window so's you can see the trail. Keep an eye out for Packard while I tell all of you what we're gonna do."

Ardahl settled at the window, and Colden explained, "Here's my plan to catch Packard and his bunch in the gun trap: Vince and I have extra weapons in our saddle-

173

bags so's we can each have two guns. There's a box canyon about two miles due north of here, and if we can lure Packard and his men into that canyon, it'll be a perfect setup. We'll let 'em ride in far enough to realize they're starin' at a rock wall with no way out but the way they came in, and then we'll move in behind 'em and cut 'em down quick."

"Sounds good," Franklin Kreeger declared. "And it shouldn't be any problem gettin' 'em there, 'cause I hear tell Packard's as good at trackin' as any Indian."

"I've heard the same thing," Colden responded. "That's why I know he ain't gonna have no trouble followin' me and Vince up the mountain and right here to this cabin." He chuckled, adding, "But just to make sure, we deliberately made it real easy for him to—"

"Judd!" Ardahl suddenly exclaimed. "Rider comin'! He's still quite a ways off, beyond that line of low hills, so I can't make him out none too clear."

"Just one man alone?" Colden queried, immediately shoving his chair back from the table and heading for the window.

"Yep."

Taking the glasses from Ardahl's hand, Colden muttered, "Aw, it must just be some guy headin' somewhere by himself. Couldn't be Packard. He'll come with a good-sized posse, I'm sure." Looking through the field glasses, he focused on the lone rider, then swore.

"What's the matter, boss?" asked Vince Denning.

"It *is* Packard! I can tell by his size and build! Can you beat that? He's comin' after us all by his lonesome!"

"Good!" Denning rejoined. "Let's just blow him to kingdom come when he rides up."

"Not on your life," Colden countered, idly fingering the jagged scar on his face. "He's got too much skill with a gun, and he don't kill easy. I still want to lure

him into a trap at the box canyon, 'cause it's the only
sure way to kill him without any of us becoming casual-
ties. If we try to take him on here, sure enough he'll
get some of us, and I need all you fellas to take over the
mines. Come on. Let's go."

Waiting till Packard had ridden behind a hill, the
outlaws hurriedly left the cabin, leaving the door to
swing in the breeze, and mounted up. Colden and his
men then spurred their horses and galloped north.

Ten minutes later, Jess Packard spotted the cabin as
he rounded a rock formation. Edging back around for
cover, he dismounted and studied the place, which
seemed to be deserted. Finally he cautiously approached
the cabin and found it unoccupied, but he could tell
that whoever had been there had not been gone long.
And judging from the way the inside of the cabin looked,
it was likely that the occupants had been the outlaws.

Returning outside, Packard studied the ground surrounding the cabin, finding the fresh hoofprints on the north
side. He determined there were at least five, perhaps six,
riders. That meant Colden had picked up some more men.

Swearing, the ex-sheriff ran back to his mount and
had just reached it when he saw a lone rider coming
along the trail he had just ridden. Horse and rider
momentarily disappeared in a dip in the road, then
they topped the hill, and when the sun shone on the
rider's long auburn hair, he knew it was Angie McGuire.

Angie spotted him and waved, then put her horse
into a canter and soon reached Packard's side. Sliding
from the saddle, she said brightly, "Hello, Jess."

Frowning at her, he asked harshly, "Angie, what are
you doing here? It's far too dangerous. You could get
yourself shot. Colden and Denning have picked up
three or four more men."

The redhead's blue eyes shone with love as she stepped

close to him and countered, "I couldn't let you face those outlaws alone. I have a gun in my saddlebag, and I know how to use it. I borrowed it from Charlie."

Looking down at her and fighting his desire to take her in his arms and kiss her, Packard asked, "Is the horse Charlie's, too?"

"Uh-huh."

"Does Charlie know you borrowed his gun and his horse?"

Angie looked at the ground, then met his gaze again. "Well, I suppose he does by now," she answered wryly, unsuccessfully suppressing a smile.

Packard felt the powerful magnetism that existed between them. He had felt it the first time he had met her in Aurora, but he had struggled against it because of Monica Wood. But now Monica was out of his life, and there was no obstacle in his way. His heart was beating wildly as he admonished, "Young lady, you've been naughty. If I were your father, I'd scold you."

Angie stepped closer, and they were just inches apart. Tilting her head back, she looked into his eyes and, a provocative smile on her lips, murmured, "Well, since you aren't my father and therefore can't scold me, what *will* you do?"

Packard looked in the redhead's eyes, and giving in to his desire, he folded her into his arms. "Since I can't scold you," he half whispered, "I guess I'm going to have to kiss you."

Their lips blended in a fiery kiss, and he could feel her throbbing heart, matching the beating of his own, against his chest. The kiss ended, but they stayed locked in each other's arms.

Pulling back just enough to look up into Packard's face, Angie declared, "Jess, I have a confession to make."

"About what?" he asked, devouring her with his eyes.

"I lied to you."

His dark eyebrows arched. "You did? When?"

"This morning. At the way station. I told you I was sorry that Monica broke your engagement . . . but I'm really not sorry at all. I'm glad!"

Grinning, the ex-lawman breathed, "I'm not sorry, either," and kissed her again.

Packard finally broke the kiss and, cupping her face in his hands, told her, "I want you to go back to the Tigman place right now and wait for me there. I have to handle these outlaws alone. I'd never forgive myself if anything happened to you."

"But, Jess—"

"Please, Angie. It's bad enough having to carry the burden of knowing I killed my own brother; if you were to die because of me, I couldn't live with it."

"I understand," the redhead said softly. She obediently mounted up. Her eyes were moist as she looked down at him and told him, "I'm falling in love with you, Jess. I didn't think I'd ever let myself feel this way after being so hurt, but I guess I started falling for you since the first moment I saw you on Pine Street."

Smiling, he replied, "It was the same for me. I couldn't admit it to myself then because of Monica, but you won my heart from the start."

Angie smiled at him, then wheeled her horse around and trotted away. She looked back over her shoulder once, then put the animal to a gallop.

After watching the redhead's ever-diminishing figure for a long moment, Packard mounted up and took off after the outlaws.

Judd Colden and his gang had stashed their horses in a far corner of the box canyon, ensuring that Packard would follow the hoofprints far enough in, and were hiding in the thick brush at its mouth. Each man armed with two revolvers, Colden, Denning, and Kreeger were

on one side, while fifty feet away on the other side were
Reedy, Hice, and Ardahl.

Soon they heard the sound of a slow-moving horse,
and the gang leader peered southward and saw Jess
Packard, who was leaning from the saddle, studying the
ground and following the hoofprints into the deadly
trap. Signaling the three men on the other side of the
canyon's mouth, indicating that their prey was almost
within reach, Colden tensed, eagerly waiting to drill
the ex-lawman full of hot lead.

The curve of the rugged land disguised the box canyon, making it appear to be just another of the count-
less rocky canyons weaving through the High Sierras
that always intersected with more canyons but never
ended. Gun in hand, Packard cautiously nudged his
mount forward into the mouth of the canyon. As the
ex-sheriff continued farther into the canyon, studying
the tracks, he followed around a bend and left the
canyon's mouth behind.

Waiting until they were sure Packard would not hear
them, the outlaws stepped out from behind their cover
and ran into the canyon. By the time they reached the
bend, Packard had begun heading toward the massive
rock wall that would soon confront him. Colden and his
men slunk forward, finally hunkering behind a jumble
of rocks and boulders, ready to block Packard's escape
and blast him from the saddle with a dozen guns.

Finally lifting his eyes, Packard found himself facing
a sheer, fifty-foot wall looming less than seventy yards
away. Quickly his eyes darted back and forth, taking in
the granite shoulders rising on both sides to meet the
wall at the corners, and it hit him like a bolt of lightning: *He was in a box canyon!*

Realizing he was in a trap, the seasoned lawman
pulled his feet from the stirrups and dived for the
ground. As he left the saddle, a dozen guns opened

fire, echoing off the canyon walls, and Packard felt a bullet pluck off his hat and leave a burning trail on his left temple. Hitting the ground and rolling behind a knee-high pile of rocks, he heard bullets ricocheting off the stones with earsplitting, high-pitched whines. He felt warm blood trickling down his cheek, and his head was spinning as though he had been kicked by a mule.

Above the roar of the blazing guns, Packard thought he heard a loud whooping, then the gunfire abruptly died out. The ex-lawman cautiously looked over the rocks to see Joaquin Jim and at least two dozen Paiute warriors holding rifles on the six outlaws. Colden and his men had dropped their guns at the chieftain's command and were standing with their hands over their heads.

Joaquin Jim signaled for his men to dismount. Remaining on his horse, the chieftain squinted toward Packard and called, "Are you all right, Sheriff Packard?"

Though his head was still throbbing and buzzing, Packard called back, "Yes! I'm all right!"

The chieftain gazed over the faces watching him warily. Joaquin Jim then stared unwaveringly at the gang leader, whose face bore the distinctive jagged scar, and demanded, "Are you Judd Colden?"

Colden's face stiffened with terror, and it was obvious that he fully expected to pay for the murders of the Paiute boys.

Saying no more to Colden, the chieftain then asked, "Which one of you is Vince Denning?"

Denning did not identify himself. Joaquin Jim peered intently at the five faces, then asked again, his tone menacing, "Which one is Vince Denning?"

The other four exchanged fearful glances. Clearly none of them wanted to be mistaken for Denning, who was being singled out, along with Colden, and almost in unison they pointed to their cohort, identifying him for the chieftain. Denning swore at them, calling them traitors, but they merely looked down at their feet.

Joaquin Jim abruptly barked an order in the Paiute language. Without warning, the warriors took aim at Reedy, Hice, Ardahl, and Kreeger and opened fire. The four men went down screaming as bullets ripped into their bodies, and in seconds they were dead. Colden and Denning stood aghast, their eyes bulging, although they kept their trembling hands high above their heads.

Sliding from his horse, the chieftain strode over to Packard. Packard felt a bit light-headed, but he concentrated hard as the chief explained that he had returned to his village shortly after the ex-sheriff had left. Learning of the boys' murders and of Packard's pursuit of the killers, he had armed his warriors and ridden into Aurora, where he had been told by the deputies of Packard's resignation as well as of the location of Colden's cabin. Wanting justice done, Joaquin Jim had followed with his men to help Packard.

As the ex-lawman dabbed at his wound with a bandanna, he responded, "I am very grateful for all your help, Joaquin Jim. But why did you spare Colden and Denning and kill those other outlaws."

The Indian looked surprised. "These men tried to kill you. Joaquin Jim has fixed it so they cannot try again. We spared Colden and Denning because you need them to clear your name."

Packard was puzzled. "How did you know that?" he asked. But before he could get an answer, a rider came galloping into the canyon . . . a rider with long auburn hair.

Angie McGuire leapt from her saddle and ran to Packard. Seeing the bloody bandanna held to his head, she gasped, "Jess, are you all right?" Assured that it was only a flesh wound, Angie explained that she had met up with the Paiutes shortly after leaving Packard and had told Joaquin Jim what was happening, urging him to hurry to the ex-sheriff's aid. She had described Colden to the chief in detail but found Denning much harder to describe. She could only tell Joaquin Jim to be sure to identify them and take them alive so they could clear Packard's name.

Smiling, Packard murmured, "I should have guessed it was you, darling." Packard's face then stiffened, and he turned to the two outlaws, snapping, "I'm in no mood for games, so you better tell me the truth right off. What was my brother doing at the big house the night of the shoot-out? Was he in league with you, or did he come by his extra money the way he said he had—from poker?"

Both men bristled, and Colden snapped, "We ain't tellin' you nothin'!"

"Okay," Packard said flatly, shrugging. Turning to the chieftain, he said, "They're all yours, Joaquin Jim. Just so you know, it was Colden who murdered those three Paiute boys, but Denning probably urged him on. Do what you want to with them."

Abruptly, Denning cried, "I'll tell you whatever you want to know!" The outlaw quickly stated that Alex had indeed won the money in poker games and was not in cahoots with the gang at all. The younger Packard had spent so much time with Denning because he was trying to get his old friend to leave the gang and get an honest job.

Denning then confessed that the day the Packard brothers had ridden out for their hunting trip, one of Troop's men had seen them and reported it to Troop. The mineowner decided to take advantage of the sheriff's absence by having Colden and Jocko Bane kill a couple of Winnemucca men.

The outlaw went on to explain that young Curt Sibley had been sickened by all the bloodshed going on, and when he had learned that Colden was planning a gun trap to kill Sheriff Packard, he went to Alex and told him about it.

"Sibley, eh?" Packard mused.

"Yeah," Denning confirmed. "The evening of the shoot-out, Alex came runnin' to the big house to plead with me to put a stop to the gun trap. We was arguin' about it when we saw you comin' toward the house." He paused, then added, "Maybe you heard a shout just before the shootin' started."

"Matter of fact, I did."

Denning nodded. "That was Alex tryin' to warn you that the gang was gonna open fire on you." He briefly glanced at Colden, then continued, "I guess it don't matter now to tell you. It was Judd who killed Alex. The first shot you heard was Judd puttin' a bullet into your brother's stomach."

Colden glared at Denning as Packard's mouth fell open. The ex-lawman felt Angie squeeze his arm, and he gasped, "You're telling me that I didn't shoot Alex?"

Denning's face registered surprise. "You mean you thought *you* shot him? You thought you killed your own brother?"

"Yes, I did," Packard answered quietly. "It's been eating away at my gut."

Fighting back his emotions, Jess Packard reached for the redhead and held her tightly in his arms, whispering into her ear, "Oh, Angie! I'm suddenly a thousand pounds lighter! Now I feel that I can live again."

His relief washing over him like a cleansing bath, Packard turned back to the others. Looking into the chieftain's black eyes, he said, "Joaquin Jim, I hope that you will abide by our treaty and let these men be punished according to the white man's laws. I assure you, Judd Colden will hang for murdering the boys."

Nodding, Joaquin Jim responded, "I am satisfied that justice will be done."

The outlaws were bound tightly and put onto their horses, and then the Paiutes, Angie, and Packard mounted up and rode out of the box canyon, leaving the bodies of the other outlaws to the vultures and coyotes.

The next day a huge crowd collected in front of the sheriff's office, ringing a buckboard that had been drawn in front. Standing in the wagon bed was Vince Denning, who confessed to the townspeople the whole story. Denning, who would be spared the rope but sent to prison, made sure everyone understood that Alex Packard was innocent of any wrongdoing. Lola Packard stood beside her brother-in-law and wept with relief to hear her late husband's name cleared.

When the deputies had returned Denning to his cell, Derek Wood stepped up to Jess Packard and apologized on behalf of the entire town, asking if he would once again wear the sheriff's badge. A loud cheer rose from the throng as Packard took the badge from Wood and pinned it to his shirt. A grinning Packard gazed down at Angie McGuire, who stood on Packard's other side, looking up at him with pride and love on her face.

People came by one by one, apologizing personally for doubting him, as well as his brother. Finally Monica Wood approached Packard, turning a dazzling smile on him. "Jess, darling, you have an apology coming from me, too. I'm sorry that I doubted you." She glanced briefly at Angie, and for a fleeting moment the smile left her face, then asked Packard, "Could we talk? Alone?"

His face stiff, Packard replied, "Anything we have to say can be said right here."

Visibly uncomfortable, Monica cleared her throat and

murmured, "I wanted to tell you that I still love you, and I want to reinstate our engagement."

After gazing down at Angie, close beside him, Jess Packard stared at Monica and said coldly, "If you really loved me, you would have believed in me. When you turned on me, you destroyed my feelings for you." Slipping his arm around Angie's waist, he added, "I've found my true love, Monica."

Turning his back on the blonde, who flushed with anger and stomped away, Sheriff Jess Packard folded the beautiful redhead in his arms, looked deep into her eyes, and kissed her soundly.

THE BADGE: BOOK 23
DEATH BADGE
by Bill Reno

Russell B. James has wanted but one thing in life: to wear a badge. But his dream can never be realized, for Russ is an ex-convict who spent two years in prison after being pressured by his cousins, the infamous Frank and Jesse James, into transporting stolen money. His past—and his family name—will forever haunt him.

After Russ is unfairly accused of consorting with his notorious relatives, he is fired from his job as a railroad guard and heads for Denver to look for work. Traveling on the same train is U.S. Deputy Marshal Al Wells, whose life Russ once saved, and the murder witness that Wells is guarding, beautiful Susan Wayland. When Wells is killed by men determined to assassinate Susan and prevent her from testifying, Russ's dream is finally fulfilled. He puts on the deputy marshal's badge and assumes the role of a federal lawman in order to get the young woman to safety.

The journey is a challenge even to a skillful marksman and fighter like Russ. Unknown assailants lurk everywhere, and danger is around every curve—including those of his stunning companion. In the course of the trip Russ falls in love with Susan, but the price of that love may be more than anyone should have to pay.

Read DEATH BADGE, on sale July 1991 wherever Bantam paperbacks are sold.